PENGUIN METRO READS
CAN LOVE HAPPEN TWICE?

Ravinder Singh is a bestselling author. His debut novel *I Too Had a Love Story* has touched millions of heart. *Can Love Happen Twice?* is his second book. After spending most of his life in Burla, Orissa, Ravinder has finally settled down in Chandigarh. Having worked as a computer engineer for several years at some of India's prominent IT companies, Ravinder is now pursuing his MBA at the world-renowned Indian School of Business, Hyderabad. Ravinder loves playing snooker in his free time. He is crazy about Punjabi music and loves dancing to its beat. The best way to contact Ravinder is through his official fan page on Facebook. You can also write to him at itoohadalovestory@gmail.com or visit his website www.RavinderSinghOnline.com.

Can Love Happen Twice?

RAVINDER SINGH

Penguin
metro reads

PENGUIN METRO READS

Published by the Penguin Group

Penguin Books India Pvt. Ltd, 7th Floor, Infinity Tower C, DLF Cyber City, Gurgaon 122 002, Haryana, India

Penguin Group (USA) Inc., 375 Hudson Street, New York, New York 10014, USA

Penguin Group (Canada), 90 Eglinton Avenue East, Suite 700, Toronto, Ontario, M4P 2Y3, Canada

Penguin Books Ltd, 80 Strand, London WC2R 0RL, England

Penguin Ireland, 25 St Stephen's Green, Dublin 2, Ireland (a division of Penguin Books Ltd)

Penguin Group (Australia), 707 Collins Street, Melbourne, Victoria 3008, Australia

Penguin Group (NZ), 67 Apollo Drive, Rosedale, Auckland 0632, New Zealand

Penguin Books (South Africa) (Pty) Ltd, Block D, Rosebank Office Park, 181 Jan Smuts Avenue, Parktown North, Johannesburg 2193, South Africa

Penguin Books Ltd, Registered Offices: 80 Strand, London WC2R 0RL, England

First published Penguin Metro Reads by Penguin Books India 2011

ISBN 9780143417231

Typeset in Bembo by SURYA, New Delhi
Printed at Thomson Press India Ltd, New Delhi

A PENGUIN RANDOM HOUSE COMPANY

To my readers who love me,
believe in me and encourage me to write more.
This one is for you.

Before You Read Further . . .

Now that I have completed this book, which is only a short while away from coming out in print, it is important for me to tell you who I am and why I am writing this book.

I am an author by chance. A lot of good and bad things happen in life, just by chance. My first book *I Too Had a Love Story* was an outcome of the tragedy in my life and, honestly, was my reason to survive. Never before had I thought of becoming an author. But I am blessed to share that the book that I wrote as a tribute to my girlfriend has fetched immense love and respect from my readers.

The impact of the story on my readers was such that I received (and keep receiving) uncounted emails, scraps and messages from them. They share their respective love stories and I must say that they literally pour out their hearts while writing to me. Sadly for me, many of those writings have sad endings. They feel at peace after sharing their true stories with me. But having read those messages I realized that you don't always need a wild truck racing madly on the road to kill a love story, the way it happened in my story. Most of the time I found that people themselves have killed their love stories. They call it 'break up'.

The ever-increasing numbers of such emails made me comprehend that, these days, 'Heartbreak' is a far more rampant disease than 'Heart Attack'. And, unfortunately, insurance covers just the latter. This is the very reason behind writing this book.

So is this book again my true story?

I believe that every fiction is inspired by a true story. Maybe this is my story, maybe not, maybe it is only partly my story, maybe not, maybe it is an amalgamation of several stories that my readers write to me, maybe not. I don't want to reveal how much fact and how much fiction there is in my story. Rather, I want you to discover it with your own imagination. But I will leave you with this one truth, and believe me when I say this: it is our generation's true story. This is the prime reason I have dedicated this book to my readers. As you read this story I want you to put yourself in the shoes of Ravin and enjoy reading your own story.

Prologue

What can you say about a guy who lost his girlfriend by the time the two of them were to exchange their engagement rings?

That he plunged into the deepest ocean of trauma? That, for whatever happened, he lost his faith in God? That he was so madly immersed in the love of his mortal girlfriend that, after she was gone, forever, he wrote an immortal love story in her memory?

Or maybe that, after a long interval of time, one day, love knocked at his door once again?

One

Dusk had fallen when Amardeep walked out of the exit gate of the busy Chandigarh airport. A chilly winter welcomed him for the very first time to 'The City Beautiful'. The evening was even more beautiful for it was Valentine's Day. Love was in the air and red was the colour everywhere. The temperature must have been close to 4 degrees. Adding to the winter chill was the cool breeze which was blowing that evening, compelling the just-arrived passengers to pull out their jackets.

Enjoying the initial few moments, Amardeep let his body feel and embrace the cold surrounding him, but he could not bear it for long. Soon he pulled out his jacket and zipped it up till his neck. The foggy breath that he exhaled was visible. It was that cold.

At the exit door, the constant announcements, the honking taxis, the crazy relatives and the masses of passengers all made the place chaotically noisy. A few taxi drivers had besieged Amardeep, offering him a paid ride. Amid the hustle-bustle of getting a passenger one of the drivers almost lifted his bag and asked,

'*Kithey jaana hai, paaji?*'

Amardeep quickly retaliated by snatching his luggage back from him. With this gesture he signalled his disagreement to take a cab.

He then made his way out of the gathering. In one hand he had his favourite *Economic Times* and a half-filled water bottle while in the other he held the handle of his wheeled bag which he rolled in tandem with his walk. He walked up till the parking lot where there was not much of a crowd. The place was calm. Underneath a row of tall lamp posts, there stood scores of cars. Amardeep perched his back against the bonnet of the first car in the series. By then the exposed parts of his body had turned cold. He placed the newspaper on the bonnet and put the water bottle over it to prevent it from flying off with the wind. Looking here and there in search of someone, he rubbed his cold palms against each other and breathed out a puff of warm air to warm them up.

Seconds later, he pulled out his cellphone from the pocket of his jeans and switched it on to make a call.

'Yes, I am at the parking lot,' he said and kept describing the whereabouts of the place he was at, until a black Santro stopped right in front of him.

'Raam j-i-i-i-i-i!' shouted someone as the door of the car opened.

It was the nickname with which Amardeep had been baptized during his college days, and it still hadn't left him.

His friends Happy and Manpreet had come out of the car to embrace Amardeep. A round of warm greetings and smiles occupied the next few minutes. It was nostalgic for them to meet each other after so long. The last time they had been together was during their first reunion which had happened almost five years back. Maybe that's why they couldn't help themselves from celebrating this moment with a long, melodramatic hug. It might have been bizarre for others to watch the three guys hugging each other on a Valentine's Day evening!

The headline on the fluttering *Economic Times* under the half-filled bottle over the bonnet of the car behind them read, 'Delhi High Court finally does away with Section 377; Homosexuality now legal in India.'

Moments later, while Happy dumped Amardeep's luggage in the rear of the car, Amardeep took the back seat and relaxed. Happy started the vehicle and Manpreet turned off the music system to enable further conversation. They talked to each other for a while as Happy drove the car out of the airport towards the city.

After a drive of some fifteen kilometres, Happy stopped the car in front of a local Internet cafe.

'What happened, dude?' probed Manpreet.

'Nothing much—just a quick email!' Happy answered undoing his seat belt. 'Give me ten minutes and I will be back.'

Amardeep tried to understand the criticality but then stepped back from asking any question. He knew Happy's strange nature of giving preference to little things.

In Happy's absence, Manpreet and Amardeep chatted for a while.

Happy returned quickly. He didn't even take ten full minutes.

'That was fast,' Amardeep acknowledged.

'I told you it's going to be quick.' Happy chuckled. Without revealing much detail, he started the engine again.

Some time passed and gradually they became silent. Happy kept driving. Each of them had the same thought running in his mind. But Happy was first to speak.

'I am missing him.'

No one said anything for a few moments.

Then Amardeep put his hand on Happy's shoulder.

'We all are missing him. And this reunion is for Ravin,' said Amardeep.

'He is right,' said Manpreet in response. 'We are here for good. We are here for Ravin. Let us cheer for this reason instead of being sad.'

A ray of hope passed across their faces, giving way to a euphoric smile in addition to a steely resolve that they would help their friend.

Happy pressed the accelerator, signalling that he was doing well. Manpreet increased the volume of the music system in the car.

A little later Happy shouted against the volume of the song being played, encouraging everyone's mood.

'Has anyone of us been on a radio channel ever?'

'No!' came the responses in unison.

'Has anyone ever seen what a radio station looks like from inside?' Happy's voice roared further.

'Hahaha . . . No . . . no . . .' followed the answers again in unison, this time accompanied with laughter.

'Doesn't matter, as long as we are clear about what we are going to do. This one is for Ravin hu-u-u-u-u-u-u-u-u . . . hu-u-u-u-u-u!' completed Raamji.

Happy then pointed his finger towards the glove compartment beneath the dashboard of the car and asked Manpreet to open it and look for an envelope. Manpreet found it and picked it up. It was a nicely packed white envelope with the logo of a prominent radio station embossed on the top left corner: Superhits 93.5 RED FM . . . Bajaate Raho! Inside was an invitation letter which Manpreet opened with twinkling eyes. He lit the roof light of the car and began reading the letter out loud for everyone's sake.

'This Valentine's Day evening Superhits 93.5 RED FM is delighted to host the talk show with the real-life characters of the bestselling and heart-touching true romantic tale of this decade—*I Too Had a Love Story*. We at Superhits 93.5

RED FM truly consider this love story to be the equivalent of a modern-day Taj Mahal, written by a lover in the memory of his beloved. On this Valentine's Day we are proud to have on our show Ravin, who wrote and shared his love story with us, along with his good friends Happy, Amardeep and Manpreet who are again the real-life characters in the book as our guests. So tune into this Valentine's Day's special show *Raat Baaki, Baat Baaki*, only on Superhits 93.5 RED FM, the number-one FM station, at 9 p.m., to talk to Ravin and his friends, to listen to the unsaid stories behind the making of *I Too Had a Love Story* and to know what more happened in Ravin's and his friends' lives after this book got launched.'

At the same moment, somewhere in the silence of a barely visible, foggy night in Shimla, someone is sitting on the staircase in front of his room. There is a row of rooms and in front of those rooms is a huge lawn. He is wearing a heavy blanket to protect himself from the cold. He has long hair and a beard which he hasn't shaved for months. It appears he is not doing well. He sits still and his gaze is fixed on something he is holding in his hands. There is no one around him. A dead silence persists and the only audible sound is the sound of the night. Just above his head there is a dimly lit yellow bulb under which hangs a board: 'Rehabilitation Centre—Ward no. 4'.

Two

It was 8.30 p.m. when they finally parked their vehicle in the parking lot of the radio station. Everything surrounding them was invisible in the fog. Such heavy fog was not unusual at this time of year—sometime in mid-February—when winter bids goodbye in the northern part of the country. It was one such day.

The doors of their cars opened, churning the dense fog surrounding them. The chill in the air immediately attacked them and they were quick to get into their jackets. While they talked, the warm air they exhaled blended with the clouds of fog they were in.

Running the zip of his jacket up till his neck once again, Amardeep gave the others some food for thought.

'What is it, like . . . 5 degrees?'

Manpreet didn't delay. Slipping his iPhone out of his pocket, he flaunted the gadget as he consulted it and corrected Amardeep: '7.55 degrees Celsius, which is 45.59 Fahrenheit.'

Inside he felt happy that finally a moment came wherein he could fall upon his superhuman gadget. A tech-savvy guy, he seldom missed an opportunity to exercise the use of his American gadgets and enjoyed converting Indian measures into American units, all at the same time.

Snug in their jackets, jeans and leather boots, they walked towards the radio station. Their footsteps, marching in unison, stirred the hibernating silence in the parking lot.

Happy was aware who he had to meet at the station. By now he had already got a call from the radio station's event manager.

At the entrance they pushed open the black glass door. Noticing this, the security guard sitting inside hastily got into his prescribed action. He confronted them with the usual who-are-you and whom-do-you-want-to-meet questions. Holding his gun, he collected the invitation card that Happy showed him in reply. He perused through the same, letting them know that he could read.

Satisfied, he led the three of them to the couch in the reception area. While they occupied their seats, he proceeded to pass on the invitation card to the receptionist at the desk. Behind the desk, on the wall, flashed the giant brand logo: Superhits 93.5 RED FM ... Bajaate Raho! Contrary to Manpreet's wishes the receptionist wasn't that hep. But she was pretty in an innocent way and looked extremely professional.

'I hope you all are here for the *Raat Baaki, Baat Baaki* show?' she politely asked, standing up from her chair.

'Yes,' Happy turned his head and replied.

'Kindly take the corridor on your right and go straight. Room no. 3 on your right is where you need to go. Shambhavi has been waiting for you.'

Now that's a nice name—Manpreet almost said this out loud, kicking out the silhouette of the would-be receptionist from his mind and developing one of the would-be RJ host now.

Unaware of Manpreet's mischievous thoughts, Happy led the team. This was the first time they were at a radio station and they were observing the environment they were in. As they walked on the green carpet in the narrow corridor, they noticed the formal silence persisting in the radio station. The path was illuminated only with dim lights installed overhead, creating a red haze of vision. They passed a series of fluorescent room numbers which were put up on the doors.

They stopped by room no. 3. Happy quietly pushed the door open. Manpreet and Amardeep followed him in. The RJ for the show was waiting for them.

'Hello! I am Shambhavi,' a beautiful voice of a beautiful girl welcomed them.

While offering a quick handshake to the three of them, Shambhavi further said, 'I have been waiting for you.'

For his own naughty delight, Manpreet didn't allow that

handshake to be quick. He felt her hands radiating a further chill through his already cold hands.

The three of them introduced themselves to Shambhavi, and it was Shambhavi's turn now.

With a smile, she said, 'I am your host and the RJ for our show *Raat Baaki, Baat Baaki* for which you all are here tonight.'

She quickly interacted with everyone and, feeling the absence of Ravin, inquired, 'Where's Ravin?'

Her inquiry brought in a moment of panicked silence with the three guests momentarily looking at each other. And before Happy could open his mouth to reply, the door on the other side opened and a tall man came running in with some papers in his hand.

'Shambhavi, rush! You have thirty seconds to go live.'

Apparently, he was the only guy who appeared to be rushing.

'Why are you always so panicky, Shantanu?' said Shambhavi, showing some attitude and flaunting her confidence. 'Relax!'

Shambhavi quickly gathered the spilled-over papers on the table beside her and walked inside the audio room, commanding Shantanu, 'Take care of them and explain everything in detail. Once Ravin is here we will go live. Keep going fast.'

Giving due acknowledgement to her guests she baulked for a split second to give an excuse-me-I-have-to-rush-see-you-inside look. As she walked in, the others kept looking at her. Happy swallowed his incomplete answer back to the bottom of his throat.

Through the giant glass window they could see the entire inside of the audio room. It had a big table in the centre taking up almost the entire space of the room which was the only duly lit part of the room. The table was decked with various hi-tech audio gadgets, with headphones installed overhead. Watching all this felt new.

The next fifteen-minute conversation with the three of them brought in further disappointment for Shantanu—he was told something which was not in the plan.

'What?' He didn't believe what he heard and cross-checked one more time. He heard the same answer again from Amardeep.

'Then how are we going to have this show?' demanded Shantanu, agape.

He invested a minute to think of something and then—probably when nothing appeared in his mind—he did what he was good at.

He rushed.

Back in Shambhavi's audio room, he cautiously pushed open the door and poked his head in.

Just like any given day, Shantanu's fear was ignored by her. Quickly muting her microphone while there was a song running in the background, she blasted at him, 'You always come with panic attacks. Now you would say that we would need to carry on the show without Ravin. Isn't it?'

'Aaa . . . yes.' The words came haltingly out of his mouth, followed by 'But . . .'

And Shantanu's so-called 'but' remained incomplete when Shambhavi ignored Shantanu's reasoning and, instead, asked him to send the three of them in.

'I will handle it. Let the producer know that Ravin is not in and we are going without him.'

That's all she had to say. Apparently, for Shambhavi, this was yet another show—part of her daily job—which she had to complete on time before leaving for the day. That's it.

Shantanu realized there was no point in explaining things to Madam Hitler and therefore he sombrely walked back.

'Sir, she is in the habit of getting carried away and not listening to me,' Shantanu stated, expecting them to understand him.

Happy smiled and stood up to comfort Shantanu. 'Relax! We will handle this inside. Don't worry.'

As the three of them looked inside the audio room from the giant glass window Shambhavi waved for them to enter.

They obeyed, and entered.

Three

'All right, guys. Pull your socks up. We are going live in thirty seconds.'

Shambhavi broadcasted just after she dictated a few dos and don'ts to the three of them and handed them a few questions she would be asking them during the show. Interestingly, she didn't check in case her guests had any further queries. The guests surely anticipated the chance to ask questions and get clarifications.

'*Oh teri!*' Manpreet's jaw almost hit the ground. A sliver of ice made its way into his adrenaline, freezing the blood in his veins. Amardeep raised his eyebrows, and thought to himself: Dude! What the hell are you up to? Happy simply smiled. Manpreet raised his little finger, signalling that, all of a sudden, he needed to pee. Amardeep blinked his eyes in anger. Manpreet's little finger settled down.

'3 . . . 2 . . . 1 . . . and go. Hello-o-o-o-o Chandigarh!

How a-a-are you doin-n-ng? I wish you all are in pink and rocking as usual. And as usual you are listening to your own RJ Shambhavi on our prime-time show *Raat Baaki, Baat Baaki*. Hmmm . . . *To shuru karte hain hamaara ye pyaara sa* programme with my special wish to each one of you on this day. A ver-r-r-ry happy-y-y-y Valenti-i-i-ine's Day-y-y-y to you. Hahaha . . . Well, since morning I've been feeling so nice. Everything around me is just coloured in red. There is love in the air: outside in the park, on the roads, in the cafeterias and here in my room as well. *Har jagah bas pyaar hi pyaar chhaaya hua hai*. I am so excited celebrating this day. I wish plenty of love stories come true this Valentine's season and I wish today ends on a very special note for each one of you. And I am here to make this day far more special for you because Superhits 93.5 RED FM now brings you the real-life characters of the love story which has touched thousands of hearts by now. Yes, I am talking about the bestselling novel and true love tale *I Too Had a Love Story*. And soon you are going to talk to the actual people who were part of Ravin's story. So don't go away and enjoy the spirit of love when we return. Stay tuned.'

She zip-zap-zoomed her lines with practised ease, like a news reader reading from a teleprompter, but whatever she said was completely improvised. She was perfect, energetic and mind-blowing. That's what Manpreet, Amardeep and Happy felt.

As she ended those lines, she scrolled some keys up,

playing a song, after which she muted the microphone she had been using.

The first song to be played on the show was the romantic English number 'Paint My Love'.

Manpreet almost stole a moment to regain his lost breath. As he moved closer to Shambhavi, he requested, 'Instead of thirty seconds can you please let us know a minute in advance? Last one was too fast.'

Shambhavi beamed her smile with her comforting message, 'Sure.'

Happy was trying to cope with the sudden truth of the moment that all of Chandigarh would now be listening to them and that all of a sudden they would become so vulnerable.

Soon all of them were seated around the big circular table. Happy sat on the right of Shambhavi and Amardeep towards her left. Manpreet occupied the seat opposite her. The entire audio system, which Shambhavi had been operating, was in front of her. There was a monitor on which she selected the songs and the ads she was going to play. There were microphones which were centrally placed in a way that everyone on the table could speak into them comfortably. While the three friends were cautious, Shambhavi was in her carefree and ultra-confident mood. One more hour to go and the day's job would be over and she would leave for home. She wasn't very bothered about whether Ravin would turn up or not.

On the last few lines of the song, Shambhavi slew the volume and moved a few keys on the music console.

When they went on air again, Shambhavi introduced Happy, Manpreet and Amardeep to her listeners, saying that she would start the show with the real-life characters of the book and end it with the author.

Outside the radio station, Shambhavi's voice was reaching almost every listener. This 9 o'clock show had been a big hit in the city, especially among the youngsters. But that night this show turned more special, for it was dedicated to this city's bestselling author whose debut novel people had read multiple times. For over a week there had been advertisements on this radio station for this show.

As forecasted, Superhits 93.5 RED FM saw the TRP scale surging. Every other minute more and more radios were tuning in to this station's frequency: the radios in those vehicles stuck in the heavy fog, moving inch by inch on the roads of Chandigarh; the radios in each and every hostel room of Chandigarh's Punjab University; the radios in hundreds of cellphones across the city.

As soon as the song ended, Shambavi sprang into action. This time she gave Manpreet a good sixty seconds to prepare himself.

'And before we talk to them, let me just recap Ravin's story as he narrated it in his first book. The four friends— Happy, Manpreet (well known as MP among his friends), Amardeep (well known as Raamji) and Ravin—get together in Kolkata to mark their first reunion after college. In one of their conversations they decide to take up the next big subject of marriage seriously. Taking a cue from their discussion, later, Ravin creates his profile on a matrimonial website, on which he finds Khushi. Ravin lives in Bhubaneswar and Khushi in Faridabad. Gradually, both Ravin and Khushi get to know each other through their interaction over the phone and in online chatrooms. Soon, they fall in love. In their courtship of eight months Ravin happens to see Khushi on just two occasions in person; yet their mutual attraction was so strong that both of them expressed, to their respective parents, their desire to marry each other. Both sets of parents met each other and finalized their engagement and marriage. On 14 Feb. 2007, that is, exactly five years back, Ravin and Khushi were to exchange their rings. But fate had planned its own twist. Five days prior to their engagement day, Khushi's office cab met with an accident. Unfortunately, that accident proved fatal for Ravin's Khushi. Three months later, to cope with his big loss, Ravin decided to write a tribute to his Khushi. And this is how he penned down his debut novel *I Too Had a Love Story.*'

She paused for a while and then continued, 'It is such a touching tale but then we are proud of Ravin that he was able to share his story and tonight we are going to celebrate the spirit of his courage. So let's cheer up and go straight to Ravin's friends who are in our studio today.'

'So, Happy, how do you feel about being a part of this book? And tell us more about your friendship with Ravin. Did it happen just the way it is mentioned in the book?'

Oh, so Shambhavi has read the book, Raamji thought to himself.

'Before I answer that, here is my bi-i-i-g-g-g hello-o-o-o-o to Chandigarh! Hope you all are enjoying the Valentine's evening. Hmm . . . To answer your question, Shambhavi, it feels great to be a part of the book and, more importantly, to have him as a friend is the greatest of all feelings and I am sure MP and Amardeep will also agree to this.' Happy gazed at his friends sitting adjacent to him.

'Okay, let me ask Manpreet now. Tell me, Manpreet, when did you guys get to know that you were going to be a part of this book? And how did you react when you got to know that this story begins with you guys?'

Manpreet took a breath or two before he spoke. He almost began his answer with a dragging 'Hmmm . . .' But then he paused, thinking deeply, after which he got going with his reply. 'Well, interestingly, I got to know about it once the book was in the market,' he said, and smiled. His smile initiated Shambhavi's smile.

'You mean Ravin didn't tell you while he was writing?'

'No, he didn't. And had he done that I would have got my character portrayed in a better way.' Manpreet chuckled, and then added, 'Actually, I was in the US while Ravin wrote this book and got it published.'

'How about you, Amardeep?' Shambhavi turned her head to probe Raamji.

Amardeep continued smiling and clarified the picture, saying, 'Only Happy knew about it. For the rest of us it was a sweet surprise.' Giving a naughty look to Manpreet, he added playfully, 'And I believe Ravin has already projected MP's character in a much better way.'

Everyone laughed.

'All right, folks. We have just begun, and we will continue to chat more with our guests on their lives, Ravin's life and the novel *I Too Had a Love Story*. And yes, if you want to ask them your questions, call us at 9892792792. Our lines have just opened. So, Chandigarh, keep alive the spirit of Valentine's Day as we catch the first caller among you, right after this romantic song!'

Shambhavi pushed the scroller on the console, playing a new song, and muted the microphone.

'It's going well, guys,' she announced, congratulating them with a thumbs–up sign. They smiled back with hoots of 'Yeah! Yeah! Yeah!'

Shambhavi then pulled out a cigarette case from the drawer underneath the desk and offered it to the others; they declined politely.

'Excuse me, then,' she said as she made her way out of the room for a quick smoke. 'I'll be back in two minutes before the song gets over. But guys, please ask Ravin to turn up in the next fifteen minutes. The show is turning out to be bigger than what we expected.'

Amardeep wanted to say something, but Happy placed a hand on his thigh and stopped him.

In Shambhavi's absence Manpreet was the first to admire her.

'She is hot!'

Happy looked at Manpreet before turning to catch Amardeep's eye. Smiling indulgently, both gave Manpreet a look that seemed to say 'dude, you won't change'.

'Asshole,' Happy murmured.

Manpreet cautiously verified that the mute button had actually been turned on.

'What? Isn't she?' he said, trying to lighten the moment.

In a few moments Shambhavi got back in the room. She was talking on her cellphone. She was still in a euphoric mood about that evening's show being a hit. 'You guys tried to reach Ravin, na?' she asked, putting a hand over the mouthpiece of her phone before promptly resuming her conversation without bothering to wait for the answer.

No one answered but Happy gave a wry smile to his buddies, knowing that Shambhavi wasn't looking at them.

The song was about to end when Shambhavi lined up some ads to be played in tandem.

'Hey! There is our first caller,' Shambhavi announced in excitement seeing the green light blinking on the bottom right of her monitor screen.

She waited for an insurance ad to end and then proceeded to receive the call. Quickly turning off the mute button, she connected the radio station to Chandigarh. She made every listener hear that one ring before she pushed the receive button.

'Hello,' she wished the caller.

No response came from the other side.

'Hello-o-o-o. Who is this?' she asked.

This time a sweet voice replied, 'Hi Shambhavi. I am Ritika.'

'Hi Ritika, how are you doing tonight?' Shambhavi was very sweet to her, very unlike the way she was to Shantanu.

'I am doing very good, Shambhavi. I am so excited that my call got connected. I had been trying every second, since the time you said your lines are opening.' She giggled excitedly, indicating how unbelievable this experience was for her.

'So, Ritika, tell us what you do?'

'Shambhavi, I am pursuing BSc from Punjab University.'

'That's nice. So are you celebrating Valentine's Day today?'

'Yes, I am,' came the shy reply. One could sense her shy smile too.

'My boyfriend and I have been together all evening, and now we're going to have dinner together.'

'That's so nice to hear, Ritika. Okay, so quickly ask your question. Before that, tell me who you want to ask this question to.'

'Shambhavi, I would have loved to ask this question to Ravin himself but even though he is not present at this moment, I can't help myself from asking this question to Ravin's friends . . . I have read *I Too Had a Love Story* scores of times and it has become my favourite book. I have even gifted it to so many people. But every time I complete reading the book there is a sudden curiosity that takes hold of me. There is this question which hovers in my mind— but then what happened to Ravin? . . . I mean, did he ever come out of the tragedy? Where is he now, what is he doing, etc.? I want to know from Happy, Manpreet and Amardeep how their friend Ravin is doing now. I hope he is doing well.'

As soon as she completed her question the line was deliberately disconnected as per usual practice.

As the guest's question ended, Shambhavi looked up at the three friends and raised her eyebrows expectantly, with a smile on her lips.

A strange emptiness followed thereafter. Shambhavi raised her hand and moved her lips to mutely pronounce 'speak up'. She fixed her gaze at Happy, who signalled Amardeep to do the needful.

Amardeep came closer to the microphone.

'Hi Ritika. Thanks for your kind words on *I Too Had a Love Story*.' Amardeep's voice became softer as he considered what he had to say next. He continued, 'And I am sorry that I am going to give you some sad news as the answer to your question . . . Ravin . . . um . . . er . . . ah . . .' Amardeep's voice faltered.

Manpreet held Amardeep's hand supportively.

Happy lowered his eyes to the ground, facing no one. Shambhavi stared, agape. All of a sudden she had her full attention on the three friends present in her radio station and talking to Chandigarh. Amardeep's statement triggered an alarm in her mind about where her show was heading.

Taking a deep breath, Amardeep went ahead.

'It's sad news. Our Ravin . . . is not what he once used to be. He is in an unstable state of mind and not doing well. He is suffering from MDD—Major Depressive Disorder. He has been admitted into a rehabilitation centre.'

'RAVIN!! . . . RAVIN!!!!! . . . WHY DID YOU COME OUT? WHY DO YOU DO THIS EVERY TIME? . . . WARD BOY!!!!!! . . . WARD BOY!!!!!! WHERE THE HELL ARE YOU?'

The voice shatters the silence. The nurse continues to shout as she runs towards ward no. 4.

'Come, get up, child . . . Ravin, get up, my boy . . .'

She helps him get up and takes him to his bed. All this time he is silent and calm.

He opens his fist and gazes one more time at those few spoiled feathers that he has been holding in his hands for so long.

He slips them under his cushion, squeezes his hands in between his legs and sleeps.

Four

Outside the radio station, Amardeep's last statement raced across the airwaves. It was breaking news! The listeners of the show who had read Ravin's love story were in a state of shock. They chatted among themselves to reconfirm if what they heard was correct and if others were aware of this.

The traffic on the fog-smothered roads of Chandigarh almost halted. The news which emerged from Superhits 93.5 RED FM now travelled through various mobile phones as well. The flurry of phone calls and messages flying from phone to phone had surged to a level never witnessed in the past. More people tuned in, wondering what happened to Ravin. The TRP ratings for the show skyrocketed, breaking every record that any radio station would have set in Chandigarh.

There was pin-drop silence in the cars, homes and surroundings of the radio listeners. There were shocked listeners, heartbroken readers and a mass of curious people desperately waiting to listen to Amardeep's voice again.

Back in the radio room, the scene was complicated. The self-confident Shambhavi was now stunned, unable to believe what she had just heard. She simply muted the speaker and held her hand on her forehead in wonder, looking at her guests. She was angry and, at the same time, clueless.

It was unusual for any radio channel to have complete silence when the RJ and guests were present in the station. No talks, no songs, no ads—just a chaotic emptiness. The listeners were already anxious to know what had actually happened.

'Shantanu was trying to tell you this when you ignored him,' said Happy politely to Shambhavi.

Shambhavi quickly regained her feet on the ground and yelled, 'But you guys could have still revealed this to me! My entire script for this show has turned obsolete.'

Visibly angry, she lashed out at everyone in the room.

'Don't worry, we have the script with us,' said Manpreet placatingly.

'What do you mean you have the script?' she retorted.

'Allow us to speak to the listeners and you will find out,' said Happy.

Considering the current situation, Shambhavi knew she didn't have much choice. Amardeep went live again. And that was a relief to the listeners who, by now, had assumed that long break in the broadcast to be a technical glitch.

Amardeep resumed his part of the speech. He spoke

slowly, choosing his words carefully. 'Certainly . . .' he said and stopped for a while.

This single word was sufficient to alleviate the listeners' anxiety and hook them back to the show.

He continued: 'Certainly life hasn't been good to him, else the guy who taught many of us what love is wouldn't have lost his battle of life because of his loss in love.'

'You mean he could not bear the loss of his girlfriend?' Shambhavi asked that question live on radio. Everyone—both inside the radio station and outside—listened with bated breath.

'Yes,' came Amardeep's reply.

'But we thought that after penning down his tribute to his girlfriend, Ravin was successfully able to bring himself back to life.'

'Yes, he was,' Happy repeated.

'Then? What happened then?' Shambhavi demanded in an interrogative tone, as though she hoped that whatever she had heard a few minutes back wasn't true.

'He failed to do so when something similar happened for the second time.'

There was a momentary silence. Clearing her throat, Shambhavi asked, 'Second time?'

Amardeep didn't look at her but kept his eyes glued to the microphone. He inhaled and exhaled deeply before he slowly spoke again.

'Yes . . . the second time. Not many people know this.

Years after Khushi was gone, love knocked at Ravin's door . . . for the second time,' revealed Amardeep.

Hearing this, Shambhavi smartly anounced the next songs to be played on the show and proceeded with the same. She utilized this time in understanding what was on Amardeep's mind. The four of them had a round of quick talks to answer Shambhavi's queries.

Learning what was on their agenda Shambhavi underwent a state of metamorphosis. All of a sudden she discovered a great show ahead and scribbled some ideas on to a piece of paper in front of the others. She shared how she wanted to choreograph the remaining part of the show and extracted a promise from everyone that there would be no more surprises for her. Having prepared herself, the next time they went on air, she said:

'Ravin . . . To me this is the name of a brave man. A man who fell in love with the utmost commitment to his beloved. A man who, with his pious tribute to his dead girlfriend, brought her back in this world. A man who had been brave enough to yet again allow love to make its way into his life. Though the truth of the moment is brutal, there is an untouched subject which, on this V-Day's night, we want to touch base with. Apart from Ravin's friends here on the show, no one knew that Ravin was writing his second book. A story about himself which he has unfortunately not been able to complete. And I am glad to state that our guests here on this show have got that incomplete book of Ravin's with them. Yes! For the very first time, we are going to hold a reading of Ravin's most awaited second novel—*Can Love Happen Twice?* Perhaps something like this is happening for the first time in the history of radio! So all you listeners, stay tuned to listen to this first-ever live reading of an unpublished book when we return. Till then here goes the next song for you.'

The next song occupied listeners for a couple of minutes, which made the listeners more anxious.

Outside the audio room, staff members of the radio station could be seen pressed against the glass window of the wooden door, making frantic gestures that seemed to ask: 'What the hell is going on?' Shambhavi simply smiled back and made some crazy gestures with her hands, assuring the staff members that she would handle the situation. But the crowd still remained, giving back counter-gestures.

It was a chaotic situation for the listeners of radio as well. Many of them were emotional, many had no clue of what was happening. But, overall, everyone wanted to know exactly what had happened to Ravin after Khushi and, more importantly, what series of events made him land up in a rehabilitation centre.

A lot of action followed in the next few minutes. Everything that ran in the radio station ran fast. Time was limited and a lot was needed to be done. The focus had now shifted from Ravin's first book to his second. Shambhavi picked her extension phone only to give brisk commands like: 'Come in ASAP!'

Interrupting the mutual discussion between Happy, Manpreet and Amardeep, she buzzed the bell. 'Guys! Where is the book?'

Happy picked up his bag which he had placed on the floor beside his chair and answered, 'Here.'

'All right. Who is going to read it?' Shambhavi raced with her next question.

'Hmm . . . Anyone among us,' Manpreet answered.

'Be specific. Who is going to start it?'

'I will,' asserted Happy.

Shambhavi's eyes were on her piece of paper. Her right hand was furiously jotting down the next course of action. Her left hand was busy gesticulating to the others or, at times, pushing the strands of her hair behind her ear.

'How many pages are there? I am sure you don't plan to read the entire book. How long will it take?'

Hearing no response for a while, she lifted her gaze from the paper to the three friends. As her eyes followed them, she gave a knowing smile and spoke.

'All right, I know what that silence means. You can start reading it. I will ask the programme scheduler to extend this show beyond the allocated time. We will have to take a few approvals, though. But won't the publishers of Ravin's book mind narrating the whole story prior to getting it published?'

This question brought forth a smile on the three other faces.

'Publishers won't publish an incomplete book. When Ravin gets better and is in the pink of health again, he will complete it and get it published. Moreover, Ravin hasn't signed any contract for this book yet. So, you see, we have all the liberty,' Manpreet replied.

'But for how long can it go on?'

'Hmmm . . . Say about two hours if you do not play the music and advertisements in the middle. We may even skip a few pages which we know are yet to be edited.'

'I can't do away with ads for sure, but yes, I can reduce the number of songs to a great extent,' stated Shambhavi.

Meanwhile, Shantanu came in rushing with a pen and a diary. He knew that his madam was going to give him a dictation. Before the poor chap could say even a 'Yes, ma'am', Shambhavi scolded Shantanu like an angry lioness pouncing on a helpless lamb: 'ASAP doesn't mean that you appear after five minutes!'

All Shantanu could utter was 'Madam . . .' after which his voice froze somewhere in his Adam's apple and failed to come out. Only his lips moved and puffs of air mixed with strands of saliva leaked out.

Happy wondered what made Shantanu not quit this radio channel.

'Anyway, three things!' Shambhavi dictated. 'First, call the boss and explain to him that we are stretching this show for an unknown duration.'

Shantanu again wanted to say something but, not surprisingly, was cut off before he could speak.

'Just listen! Explain to him that it is very important for our channel. Feed him the fact that Superhits 93.5 RED FM is hosting a book reading of an unpublished book and the fact that no other radio channel has ever done this. Second, check with Siddharth in the broadcast room. Ask him to get in touch with our station in other metros and broadcast this book reading there as well. He has done the vice versa for us before, and this time we need other regions to broadcast our programme. If he asks for the boss's approval, ask him to SMS me. Third, no one should leave the office before the show finishes: neither the technician, the broadcasting team, the scriptwriter, the creative department nor the ads department. I may need anyone anytime.'

Shambhavi truly was the station's star RJ, which probably gave her a lot of importance at Superhits 93.5 RED FM.

In that dimly lit radio room Happy moved to the other side of the table. Shambhavi passed the microphone to Happy and switched on the overhead focus light which fell straight on the table. The radio room turned brighter. Under the beautifully falling beam of light Happy placed the diary on the table and opened it. This very act of opening that diary appeared both heavenly—as though the diary was a holy text—and emotionally charged as well. Everyone just kept looking at the diary for it was Ravin's diary, their beloved friend's diary which contained his handwritten thoughts, and which now compensated for Ravin's absence.

The next time when they went on air Shambhavi updated all the listeners that the show that night would continue for an indefinite time and that it was going to be the very first time in their history that a show would run for an unspecified duration.

In the world outside the radio station, Ravin's fans were very much willing to listen to Ravin's story irrespective of how long the broadcast would last.

Happy started reading Ravin's second book—*Can Love Happen Twice?*

Five

A year and a half had passed since the tragic incident had taken place. Unable to cope with the misery, I was looking for a big change. Fortunately, an on-site opportunity for a project in Belgium gave a ray of hope to that much-needed change. I availed that opportunity.

It was the month of January and Brussels, the capital city of Belgium, was witnessing the last few weeks of winter. It was noon, I guess around 12.30 p.m., when I walked to my hotel room in Brussels. It was indeed a delight for me to walk into that beautiful room with lovely interiors, beautifully textured walls and an excellent lighting scheme. Even the air in there was very refreshing. It was warm inside and quite calm as well. I went ahead to explore that room, which was going to be my temporary home for the next few days, in greatest detail. As I walked in, my leather boots made that aristocratic tapping sound on the wooden floor.

The wall on the other side of the room was hidden behind a giant curtain. There was a long string dangling beside the curtain. On pulling it, the curtain parted. And the next moment took my breath away.

From behind the glass wall of the room on the eighteenth floor of the hotel Tulip Inn, Brussels looked mesmerizingly beautiful! I could see almost the entire city. My eyes were glued to the panoramic sight of a serene and cold Belgium afternoon. Scores of skyscrapers—which, while standing solidly right in front of me, also seemed to compete with each other to kiss the sky—filled my view from left to right. White smoke from various massive chimney outlets, installed on the terrace of the buildings, was coming out dreamily. Far down, I could see various road networks with the traffic racing on them.

The glass wall seemed soundproof as I could hear nothing. Yet, I imagined the sound of the fast cars on the road. I imagined the whistle of the wind that was blowing outside at that level. I imagined the voices of the people walking on footpaths. I imagined it all. I stood there for a while in the pin-drop silence of my cosy room imagining all kinds of noises. I was enjoying being there; being there almost in the sky and with the beautiful city stretching out below me.

In a few moments nature started painting everything white. Tiny flakes of snow whirled right in front of my nose. The sky at that altitude was getting swathed in a sheet of white snow. And I watched that sheet becoming gradually more dense. I could feel the magic of the weather outside. I wanted to capture the moment in pictures, but I couldn't. Then and there I wanted to write a few lines of what I was experiencing, but I couldn't leave the focus. I didn't want to lose a single second of it. Everything out there was turning to white: the buildings, the roads, the air and everything else!

I stood with my palms stretched against the glass, frozen like a statue, and watched those flakes swirling down, till they lost their individuality and became a part of the homogeneous cluster of white. I don't remember how long I stood there.

~

A telephone ring on my room's phone broke my reverie. It was Sanchit, a colleague as well as a friend, who was the only Indian whom I knew in Belgium. While he was the development lead for our project, I was the test lead. Sanchit had come on-site a month prior to me and this helped me to easily settle down in Belgium.

'Okay, see you then in half an hour,' I murmured in a daze.

Religiously following the Indian tradition of procrastinating, the so-called half an hour was stretched to one and a half hours before Sanchit finally knocked at the door.

'Hey! Hi-i-i-i!'

We were glad to see each other. We shook hands and gave each other a boyish half-hug though we'd never met this way ever when we were at our office in India.

Things change when two Indians meet abroad.

Sanchit was clad in heavy, warm clothes from head to toe.

'Wow!' he said as he walked towards the glass window and turned back to see the rest of the room, smiling appreciatively.

'How much? Hmm . . . Eighty euros per night?' he answered his own question with a witty smile.

'Yup. And not bad when the company is paying,' I answered, pulling out some Indian snacks that I had got from home. He jumped to grab his share.

In the evening we walked out of the hotel to Brussels Nord. Sanchit explained to me that 'Nord' in French meant North. Brussels Nord was the nearest station from where we were supposed to catch the metro to go to Sanchit's place. It was very cold outside. The temperature was around −2 degrees Celsius. I could barely take my hands out of my overcoat pockets. On the way, Sanchit stopped at a Pakistani shop from where he bought himself a pack of cigarettes. Meanwhile, I used the shop's ISD booth to call my parents back home and update them that I had reached safely and was doing well.

I enjoyed observing people and the vicinities we passed by. The station we were in was quite hi-tech with a three-level transport system. On the ground level ran the trains.

On the level below ran the metros. And further below ran the trams. Sanchit had a monthly pass to avail the public transport across Belgium and, on his suggestion, I too got one for myself.

While we were in the train, Sanchit updated me with various facts about Belgium. The country is bilingual. Half of the country including Brussels speaks French and the other half Dutch. Belgium is famous for Belgian chocolates, Belgian beer and Belgian girls. I was yet to check the first two facts. The last one was an omnipresent truth. Belgium has a monarchical system of governance and has legalized gay marriages. The fact that interested me most was that, taking advantage of Belgium's centralized location—the best among some of the European countries—I could easily visit the nearby countries such as France, Germany, the UK and the Netherlands.

By late evening we were at Sanchit's house. I found it to be nice and cosy, although a bit cluttered since Sanchit had washed his clothes and had placed them here and there to dry. It was a costly house, but Sanchit had taken it because his wife was supposed to join him in a week's time and he had chosen the house as per his wife's preference. At that time she was back in India.

I settled into the couch in the living-room area and he switched on the TV. Sanchit brought two cans of beer from the fridge and we relaxed for a while, enjoying the much-touted Belgian beer.

Soon our conversation moved to the official things: the client, the project, the office location, the good official things and the not-so-good ones.

We cooked dinner for ourselves after which I caught the late-night metro back to Brussels Nord. I slept in my hotel room. The glass wall on my left still remained bare without the curtain, treating me to a beautiful night-time view of the city whenever my sleep broke.

Six

The next morning I was at my client's office. It was on Zandvoorstraat in Mechelen. Mechelen is another city in Belgium and, unlike Brussels, this part of the country has a Dutch-speaking population. 'Straat' in Dutch means 'street' in English. And Zandvoorstraat was the street address of my office.

The initial few hours at my client's office passed well. Primarily, my task involved greeting everyone: meeting them, introducing myself and listening to their share of the introduction. My other important task for the day was to set up my workstation, which I successfully did by noon.

'Let's go for lunch,' Sanchit suggested. 'There is a sandwich shop nearby where most of us go.'

Unlike India, where a sandwich is more like a snack, in the West it is more of a meal. Having lived in various countries I have adapted to every kind of meal by now.

Sanchit and I joined Anthony for lunch.

Anthony Gomes was one of the various clients' point of contact for us. His job was to deploy the projects we built for him at his client's location. He was fairly pink in complexion with grey eyes and curly brown hair. It seemed he loved his wife very much. That's what I had made out from the picture of his wife that he kept on his desk. Our purpose to join Anthony was simple. He had a car and he too used to buy his lunch from the same shop. Though it was a ten-minute walk to that shop, a two-minute ride in Anthony's brand new Volvo was a far more attractive proposition than a walk. On our way to grab our lunch, I primarily interacted with Anthony.

To my surprise the eatery was actually a minibus or, to say it better, a van with no seats inside but a massive display box installed to exhibit a variety of sandwiches. Behind that display box was the service area where a fat couple was busy selling sandwiches. The place had a separate entrance and exit. The queue ran from the inside of the van to a good long distance outside, proving that this little diner was doing good business. We joined at the tail of the queue.

On Sanchit's suggestion I chose Kip Sate, a chicken sandwich with hot chillies and plenty of salad. Anthony too picked the same. We paid and moved towards the exit. While coming out, I noticed that the queue at the entrance had extended further. We sat back in the car.

As Anthony reversed his car, my eyes caught someone—

someone's back, to be precise. She was a girl, the last person in the sandwich shop's entry queue. I was riveted by her—those sleek white Puma shoes under the blue denim which ran up her legs before slipping under a black overcoat; those earphone wires which ran across her untied hair that danced in sync with her shaking head and her tapping left foot. But all these were not the reasons why I noticed her. It was her complexion that caught my attention. From a distance of about twenty feet, and the fact that she had her back towards me, I could only notice a few things about her. From the colour of her hands and hair, and the barest hint of her profile face and neck, my best guess was that she was an Indian.

I don't know why, but for some unknown reason I felt a sudden urge to look at her face. Besides, I wanted to make sure if my guess was right. But then Anthony drove the vehicle out of the spot we were in and I missed my chance.

Sanchit noticed me and then looked out of the car and then looked back at me. He raised his eyebrows questioningly.

'Nothing, ah . . . I am trying to remember the way.' That said, the three of us got busy in a conversation of our own.

Then as soon as I reached office, I got busy with my work. I had a few emails from my team back in India. By that time people back at the offshore Indian office had come in and started their work too. Belgium time is four and a half hours ahead of Indian time. During the daylight-saving months in summer, the difference decreases by an hour.

The rest of my day went in taking offshore calls and resolving a few issues. It was 6 p.m. Other than Sanchit and I, everyone else had left the office by 4.30 p.m. only. We kind of maintained the tradition of Indians working for longer hours. Having completed my work, I was waiting for Sanchit to complete his.

All of a sudden Sanchit looked at his watch and then looked at me with a stupid smile.

Then he asked naughtily, 'How fast can you run?'

Unable to understand his intention, I said, 'Why are you asking this?'

'Because we have three minutes to catch our last bus,' he shouted, leaping from his chair, flipping his laptop screen shut, slipping it into the laptop bag and running towards the door.

'Faster than you-u-u-u-u!' I screamed in my client's office with no client in it.

I chased him through the door, down the staircase beside the exit and finally overtook him before we hit the road.

Sanchit's calculations had been absolutely right! The bus had just reached and we were the last two passengers to board it. Seconds before the automatic doors of the bus were to slide shut, we ran in.

We high-fived each other and laughed, the pace of our breathing slowly returning to normal.

It was a pleasure to find a few more Indians in that bus. In fact, there wasn't any Belgie—or Belgian native—apart from the driver of the bus. This proved that not just Sanchit and I, but the rest of the many Indians in Belgium also worked late at their client's location.

Sanchit introduced me to everyone. Most of the people in the bus knew each other. I learnt that they all worked in nearby places and almost all of them met each other in buses on weekdays and at each other's homes on weekends. I chit-chatted with them for a while.

A little later, I finally relaxed in one of the back seats. I was tired. Soon I was lost in my thoughts. I thought of the Belgian driver driving all the Indians back to their respective homes. I thought of the taste of the Kip Sate sandwich that I had eaten for the first time that day. I thought of that girl in front of the sandwich shop whom I had failed to see that afternoon. I thought of the weird anxiety I had had while trying to see her face. I thought of how I seemed to have felt a strange connection with her. I thought of the snow I had witnessed on my first day in Belgium and I looked up to the sky wondering when it would snow next. I thought of my mom back in India. I thought of my past. I thought of Khushi . . .

Seven

By the weekend, I had managed to find a house to rent for myself. Luckily, I found one in Mechelen itself. As my office was in Mechelen, I preferred to live there. My office was a ten-kilometre ride in the bus.

In a sixteen-floor building, my apartment was on the first floor. It was a nice place to live in. It had a spacious dining room, a nice kitchen, a cosy bedroom, a neat and clean tiled bathroom and a huge balcony. And just like the hotel room's glass wall, the entire balcony wall was made of glass with sliding doors. There was a shutter on the hood of the glass wall which automatically came down (just like an automatic garage door) when the power button installed on the adjacent wall was pressed. I loved opening up the shutter in the morning to welcome the sun's first rays and then shutting it at night before going to bed.

Every room had a heater installed to make the rooms

warm during winters. I had to use them. There was one in the bathroom as well. My house was fully furnished with a TV, sofa, dining table and bed. I loved the furniture and texture of the interiors. As soon as I got my 'white card'—an ID card for foreigners living in Belgium—I installed a nameplate at the entrance. It read my name. It is mandatory to put up your nameplate in Belgium.

In a day or two I settled down well and my life rolled smoothly. I would wake up in the morning, get ready and prepare breakfast for myself. Then I would catch the 9 a.m. bus to reach office. By 6 p.m. in the evening I would leave office and go to the gym which was near my office. At night I would cook dinner. Later, after dinner, I would have a cup of coffee and stand in the balcony with my laptop playing all the Hindi and Punjabi songs in my collection. Sometimes, standing there late into the night, I would see the red lights of the planes in the sky. I would love to believe that one of the planes among them was going to India.

Before sleeping I would pull down the balcony shutter and fall into my bed, exhausted but happy.

My apartment building didn't have a single Indian. Most of the people who lived in the building spoke either French or Dutch. English to them was a third language—more of a sign language, in fact. Sanchit lived far away from me in Brussels and his wife had joined him by now. Hence I couldn't visit his place very often. I lived alone, I cooked alone and I ate alone. There wasn't anyone to talk to because of the language barrier. Yet I did manage to cope with life's interesting challenges in Belgium. After all, they were not as brutal as the ones I had been through.

Eight

It was my second week in Belgium. One evening I was running on the treadmill in the gym. In the mirror in front of me, I noticed a face. A girl's face—as a matter of fact, a good-looking Indian girl, and she had just entered the gym. She halted right behind my treadmill. I could see her in the mirror, which also meant that she could see me as well. Perhaps she was there to say hi to a fellow Indian, which was of course me. Hence, while I ran, I kept looking at the mirror, expecting to greet her back.

However, I soon realized from her body language that she was there not to greet but to use the treadmill after I got down.

'How many minutes more?' came a question from my right.

I turned to see a young woman. She was indeed beautiful and so was her voice. Her round-necked pink T-shirt elegantly revealed a part of her poised figure. Her tight-fitting black leotards ran all the way down her firm legs. She was very fair in complexion. Her hair was drenched, probably with the sweat, and a few droplets glittered on her forehead. She was wearing a wristband. And she stood there looking at my face, munching some chewing gum, passing it from the left side of her mouth to the right and back again.

'Excuse me!' She raised her hands with a sarcastic smile on her face. It indicated that she minded my staring at her.

Honestly, I didn't have any bad intentions. All in all, I was surprised because my expectations of receiving warm wishes from another desi abroad were shattered.

'Would you mind telling me for how long you will run?'

'Sorry!' I quickly apologized for not immediately answering her question.

Then I quickly glanced at the display on my treadmill. I was still running.

'Ah . . . It's a fifteen-minute cycle and there are ten more minutes to go,' I said.

'Ten more minutes?!' She looked shocked, as though I had denied her the right to breathe for those ten minutes. She held her mouth open for a few seconds. I could easily see the colour of the chewing gum in her open mouth.

'But that's too long a wait for me.'

Oh yes, she actually said that.

What is she? Miss India? Mama's pampered girl? Didn't even say hi and expects people to jump off a running treadmill!

Gradually, her open mouth retained its previous form and the chewing resumed. Her eyes reflected unhappiness. She went back to where she had been standing earlier and waited for those year-long ten minutes to pass.

And what was I doing?

I was actually enjoying that little friction we had had. I looked at her in the mirror and could feel her restlessness. She held her hands on her waist and kept looking here and there as if she didn't care. Occasionally, she would twist her elbow and stretch her back. It was difficult for me to keep from smiling. To fuel her restlessness I increased my speed on the treadmill. As soon as I did that, she pulled out her rubber band from her hair and started stretching it only to keep herself busy.

The backward count on the display of my treadmill entered into the last few seconds of the fifteen-minute run. When exactly ten seconds were left, Madam India was standing on my head again. I was truly having a difficult time trying not to laugh out loud and focusing on my run. The treadmill slowed down automatically and suggested a cooling-off period of two and a half minutes. I ignored her and continued walking as if there wasn't anyone beside me.

As I now walked on the treadmill, I pulled out my towel from the holder in the dashboard and started wiping my arms and face. Of course she didn't like it. She kept staring at me, trying to tell me that it was my time to get down. But I continued to ignore her.

'Excuse me!' she said again.

I gave her a look.

'Your ten minutes are over, na?' she said that politely but sarcastically.

I loved that 'na' in the tail of her sentence. It contained an inherent desi touch.

'Yes, but the fifteen-minute cycle ends with a two-and-a-half-minute cool-off time.'

'This is cheating, yaar!' she blurted childishly. Her head bent on her left shoulder in total dismay. She became quiet after that.

I simply loved her expression and whatever she was doing. She was candid and honest. It was just that she didn't appear mature enough, but it was a treat to come across such innocence.

Not wanting to piss her off further, I pushed the stop button and stepped down. I thought she would thank me. But keeping up with her tendency to flout my expectations she didn't bother to do that. I noticed that her face assumed an expression of relief—she chewed on her lower lip while her eyes twinkled triumphantly. Then she quickly filled the vacancy on the treadmill and ran with great enthusiasm.

Nine

The next afternoon, I was at the same minibus-eatery which sold sandwiches to grab my lunch. Sanchit and Anthony were busy in a long conference call. Hence, I had walked alone to this place.

As usual there was a long queue, and I only added to its length.

The gentleman ahead of me initiated a conversation with me and interestingly I got quite involved in the discussion. As per the track record of my previous conversations with the local people, the subject this time was again India. More than wanting to know things about my country he was telling me what he already knew about India.

All right, so this guy was aware of who Amitabh Bachchan was, where the Taj Mahal was located in India, what the festivals of Holi and Diwali looked like. The list of the things he knew about India was longer than the queue we were both standing in.

'Voilà!' I expressed.

'Voilà' is one of the most used French words to express a there-you-are message. I was kind of getting a hold on a few French and Dutch words and loved using them wherever they aptly fit in.

I was listening to that guy's knowledge about India. But then all of sudden something—or rather, someone—grabbed my attention. From the exit of that sandwich van came out that Indian girl whom I had interacted with on the previous evening in the gym. It took her a while to notice that I was there in the queue.

I didn't expect her to talk to me.

But as usual, she did the exact opposite of what I expected. She walked straight towards me.

I lost interest in the conversation on India. The gentleman sensed it, but something in him made him keep going. I wanted to tell him: Dude, why don't you go and settle in India?

I was looking at her. The guy finally paused broadcasting his documentary on India.

'Hi!' she greeted very nicely. She looked beautiful; more beautiful than the pretty Belgian girls in the queue.

'Hello!' I replied with a smile as I crossed my arms over my chest, locking my hands firmly under my armpits.

Yes, we didn't shake hands. There were plenty of sandwiches she was holding in her hands.

'Ah . . . I am sorry for yesterday,' she said.

Finally!—I thought to myself. But, stretching my lips into a thin smile, all I said was simply: 'It's okay.'

'Actually, I had lots of things running in my mind and I was in a hurry,' she continued, trying to justify her stand.

'Relax! It happens and that's fine.'

My queue was moving ahead. I was moving ahead with it. And she was moving ahead with me.

'But why were you in a hurry?' I asked.

'I had my term exam today. I had to prepare for it,' she replied.

'Oh! So you study here?'

'Yes, I am doing my MBA.'

'So how did your exam go?'

'It went well!'

We kept talking till it was almost time for me to buy my lunch.

'Oh, by the way, my name is Ravin.'

'Hi, I am Simar,' she revealed with a cute smile.

Along with me she re-entered the van. She was with me when I bought my sandwich. I grabbed a polybag from the shop.

'You need this big a polybag to hold one sandwich?' she asked.

'Not for me.'

'Then?' I noticed her head again tilting on her left shoulder as she awaited an answer from me.

She was cute, both in her expressions and in her body language.

'For you. To hold all those sandwiches in it,' I answered, satisfying her curiosity.

She was amazed at my chivalry. She smiled.

Moments later we were out of the van. By now we had become better acquainted. She was basically from Gurgaon and had come to Belgium to pursue an MBA. She was in her second year, and her college was quite close to my office. She also had her immediate relatives living in Belgium.

'My chaachu and his family live in Brussels,' she revealed. 'I visit them sometimes.'

As per her school policy, she lived in a girls' hostel that was next to her college. It was nice to know that she belonged to a Punjabi family. I don't know if she felt nice knowing that I was Punjabi too.

That afternoon I ate my lunch walking along with Simar. Her hostel was on the way to my office. At the next crossing, where she was to take a different path, a few of her female friends stopped by in a car. They took the sandwiches from her and handed over her bag to her.

I realized that they were in a hurry and she was late in getting them their lunch. She quickly chatted with them and they drove ahead in their car. She held a white bag on her shoulder and something struck me.

We then shook hands for the very first time—interestingly, to say goodbye and see-you-soon. She was the first one to turn and move. I was still watching her, remembering something.

She took out her iPod and plugged it into her ears, and slipped her white purse on to her right shoulder. She pulled out the band and loosened her hair. I stood there noticing her walking away. All of a sudden I felt a sense of déjà vu happening. My mind told me that I had seen all this earlier and wondered where I had seen her.

It took me a while to realize.

Damn! Simar was the same girl whose back I had seen one afternoon at that same sandwich eatery!

Ten

It was my birthday and fortunately a Saturday as well. I had talked to my mom and dad early in the day. They were happy to know that all my Indian friends in Belgium were coming to my place to celebrate my birthday.

The Indian community which used to catch the evening bus had this protocol of setting up get-togethers for every big and small event. And for the sake of celebration every small event turned into a big event. On such get-togethers, the invitation used to go to almost every desi we knew by any means. Those gatherings were indeed a great opportunity to bond well together and overcome feelings of homesickness.

A day before, while we all were in the bus on our way back from office, Sanchit had announced:

'It's Ravin's birthday tomorrow, guys!!!'

And then the plan of a party at my place had been finalized even before I got off at my bus stop.

'Vasudha and Jyoti, you folks will have to come as well,' said Rishab, one of our friends in the bus.

I was proud that by now I was aware of everyone's name.

'Aiiyo, from Brussels! Ah, it's hard to come out on a weekend. Nakko ji. Need to finish some household work.' Vasudha had answered in her typical South Indian accent.

'Ask your husband to do that!' said someone in the crowd and we all started laughing.

'Hey! Everyone, get your spouses and kids as well. We're gonna have fun. See you guys tomorrow!' I said moments before we reached my bus stop.

There were some ten people, including a little kid, who showed up to celebrate my birthday. Sanchit and his wife were the most important people in the gathering. All of a sudden my empty house had become very lively. As predicted by a few, Vasudha didn't show up. And as predicted again by other few, the excuse she gave for not attending that day was that she was 'not feeling well'.

The party began. The Indians were living up to their reputation of being highly enthusiastic. There was a great deal of shouting and hooting, and many wished me Happy Birthday loudly. The little kid was crying while Bollywood songs were playing in the background. Everything was happening at the same time.

I had welcomed everyone with juices and Coke but Rishab had ignored the light drinks as he went ahead to open the refrigerator.

'Stellas!' he exclaimed and pulled out a can for himself.

'Take out some more for those who want to have beer!' I shouted.

Sanchit left the glass of juice on the dining table as he heard the word 'Stellas' and went to check the refrigerator.

'Oh boy! A dozen cans? But you don't prefer alcohol, right?' he asked, taking out one for himself.

'I got it this morning for you guys. Won't mind having one today,' I chuckled.

'Ice cream!' one of the ladies screamed as she eyed a bucket in my open fridge.

All of a sudden, I felt that everything at home had become vulnerable to inspection by the guests. Anyone could open and check out anything. My house was under everyone's control and my bathroom was under the control of the little kid who had soiled his diaper with some artistic colourings and made his mother's life more difficult.

There was absolute craziness.

Then suddenly someone screamed, 'Let's cut the cake! Hey birthday boy, come here!'

I went to the kitchen to get a knife, when Sanchit came and whispered, 'Hey, didn't you invite her?'

Busy finding the knife, I answered, 'I did. But Saturday is not off for her. She had her finance class late this evening.'

A few weeks back I got to know that Sanchit knew Simar. In fact, even before I'd told him about Simar, he had met her a couple of times at the same sandwich diner before I landed in Belgium. And in the past few days, the three of us often had our lunch together on the bench outside the diner.

Sanchit kept looking at me for a while and spoke again, 'Shall I ask you something?'

Having some idea of what he was about to ask, I laughed a bit and said, 'Dude, enjoy the drink and give me one.'

I continued hunting for the knife. Sanchit's eyes were still on me.

Trying to steer Sanchit away from the topic that was on his mind, I spoke again. 'Thanks! In case you are the one who got the cake.'

'Do you like her?' he asked with a big gulp of beer. He was looking intently at me.

'Are you crazy? There is no such thing!' I exclaimed as I found the knife under the gas stove. 'Oh, here it is. Come, let's go cut the cake.'

'Why are you avoiding my question?' Sanchit persisted.

The voices from the living room had suddenly become louder. Rishab had cracked some joke and everyone was laughing at it.

'Come on, Sanchit, we are just friends,' I said, facing the kitchen door. Sanchit was behind me.

'You like her or not?' he repeated.

I turned towards him and took a deep breath. 'You know my past very well, Sanchit . . .' I was going to continue but Sanchit cut me mid-speech.

'Yes, and because you wanted to come out of it, you left India and came here.' Sanchit's voice was louder this time.

I wasn't left with much to say. I stood still, vaguely looking at the knife which I was holding in my hand.

'Ravin, it's been a long time now. Think about your future, think about your family back home. Get yourself a life.' Sanchit gesticulated with his hands, spreading his arms wide open in the air, as he made an attempt to convince me.

Sanchit knew everything about me. He was like a brother to me. He had groomed me in the initial days of my job, and now he was supporting me quite a bit in settling in Belgium, especially in getting started at the on-site office.

I know he was absolutely justified in saying these things to me. Everyone close to me had said the same—my mom, my dad, the rest of my family and my friends. I knew they were all right. But I wasn't wrong either. I knew I wanted a change and I left India for the same, but getting another girl wasn't the change I left India for. I wanted to experience a change in terms of my daily life, my surroundings, the culture and people I interacted with. Of course I found Simar to be a nice girl, but only to interact with. It was exciting for me to see her but I never imagined myself falling in love with her.

For me love was just meant to happen once and it was forever.

How do I fill the same heart with love for someone else? Not that I never thought that way, but whenever I thought of it, I couldn't give myself an honest answer. And in the absence of any legitimate answer, I would tell myself to simply leave it all up to destiny.

'I am not saying that you should go and find happiness. All I am saying is that if happiness comes knocking at your door, then don't deny it,' he said, gently putting his raised hand on my shoulder.

His words didn't register in my mind. I stood quietly to let him finish speaking what his heart felt. Alcohol makes people speak from their hearts. Sanchit was now speaking from his.

I was yet to have my share of alcohol. I was yet to speak from my heart.

'What's cooking between you guys?' Sanchit's wife came looking for us.

'Darling! We are wondering what to cook?' Sanchit immediately responded with a smile.

'Oh, don't worry, guys. Together we will cook with whatever is available here and if there is nothing, we will order something from outside. Come on, now! Let's cut the cake!' She held my hand and took me out.

Soon everyone sang loudly in unison 'Happy Birthday to you . . . Happy Birthday to you . . .'

This was followed by a lot of clapping. The cake was cut, smeared and thrown around.

A little later we all cooked together, spoiled my kitchen together and then ate together. There was an air of warmth and fun all around. At about 8.30 p.m. I bid goodbye to everyone and was left in a messy house. It was quite early for a party to be over, but many of my guests were living in Brussels and the journey back home would take them at least an hour.

I kept staring at my messed-up house and the dirty cutlery and crockery under the kitchen sink. Cleaning up would be a huge task so I changed my clothes into a comfortable vest and shorts before I was ready to dirty my hands.

It took me close to twenty minutes to reset my living room. I was cleaning the utensils in the kitchen when my doorbell rang. I wondered if someone had returned to collect something they might have left behind. I went out to check who it was and looked through the peephole of my door.

'Shit!' I murmured.

It was Simar, with some girl.

My heartbeat had accelerated all of a sudden. Instead of opening the door I ran in. I looked at the kitchen's condition. I looked at my own condition. Then I quickly looked for my T-shirt and jeans and got back into them again. I closed the kitchen door to hide the mess in there. Only then did I unlock the main door.

'Hello,' I said, panting.

'Happy Birthday!' Simar sang, her head tilted to one side as usual.

I smiled.

'Happy Birthday!' wished the other girl and then shook my hand.

'Thank you,' I responded.

'She is Tanu, my batchmate; and Tanu, he is Ravin,' said Simar, beginning the introductions. 'He works with Pitney Bowes—you know, that blue–white coloured building, na? The one at the first right turn on the road outside our hostel?'

'Yes, yes!' Tanu acknowledged, but I could clearly see that this wasn't the first time she was getting to know this from Simar.

I welcomed them into my house. They had barely sat down when Tanu's cellphone rang. She went out to take the call. I offered her my balcony for privacy but she pointed outside, indicating that she would prefer to go out. I didn't stop her.

'I will be back in twenty minutes!' she said to Simar as she walked out.

Simar gave her a sad look. They also exchanged some strange glances and some girlish talk in sign language. I didn't understand what they were conveying to each other. It was a little uncomfortable for me to be a part of that silent conversation. Hence I took the opportunity to go to the kitchen and grab some lemonade.

By the time I returned Tanu was gone.

'What's going on?' I asked Simar, offering her lemonade but looking at the main door.

'Her boyfriend!' Simar answered. None of us felt the need to ask more or explain more.

'Sorry for this mess. My friends were here,' I mentioned.

'It's okay. Chill!' she said, squeezing her eyes shut as she pronounced *chill*.

I wondered if it was the tangy lemonade which had made her squeeze her eyes shut like that.

As we sat next to each other, I noticed that she was looking visibly uncomfortable. I assumed it had to do with the closed door and the conscious realization that it was just the two of us inside my home. I could see the discomfort on her face, in her body language, in her exaggerated smile, and even in her gestures as she repeatedly smoothened her hair.

But before she could have felt more uncomfortable, I jumped in to change the strained atmosphere. I got up from my couch and began telling her about the birthday celebrations that had taken place at home a short while back. Simultaneously, I started cleaning up the party mess.

'How come you turned up this late?' I finally asked her the question that I had wanted to ask her sometime back.

She relaxed a little. 'Arrey, I had that finance class, na. I wouldn't have been able to come at all, but the class got over half an hour early. And when I mentioned to Tanu that it's your birthday, she got all excited about eating the cake. So . . .' She left the sentence incomplete but raised her shoulders as if the rest was self-explanatory.

'Oh, so it's because of your friend Tanu that you are here.

I thought you came to wish me,' I said as I walked by her, carrying a stack of dirty dishes. I hadn't missed the opportunity to tease her.

'No. No. It's not like that!'

'Then what is it like?' I smiled back, knowing the advantage I had.

'It's difficult to come out alone, na. So I wanted Tanu to accompany . . .'

I didn't pester her further because I was trying to comfort her. I also kept cleaning the mess. She was way more comfortable now and got up from the couch to check my collection of music CDs and a few books I had on my shelf.

Eventually, we just talked as we did our own thing, our voices rising and dropping depending on where we were. Gradually, she seemed to be feeling less nervous and was laughing every now and then. She appeared comfortable talking about various things. Later, she even helped me in doing the dishes. I too wasn't embarrassed any more at the prospect of exposing my messy kitchen to her. I was enjoying her presence. I don't know why but I felt different. It all felt nice. Maybe because it had been so long since I had been with a girl in the privacy of my house at this late hour. Perhaps that's why the air around us felt so stimulating—as if it was charged with some sort of mysterious, invigorating vibes. We kept talking, after which we made some coffee and, along with the leftover cake, shifted to the balcony.

It was pleasant being there with Simar in that dimly lit

balcony and witnessing that beautiful night full of stars. I wasn't able to see her attractive face clearly but the lack of light actually made it more interesting for both of us to be out there. I don't know what exactly the darkness had to do with this, but it certainly added an overwhelming feeling to it all. Maybe it simply takes away the distance between two people who are talking and lets them be themselves. When you are not able to look into the eyes of the other person and read her thoughts, you don't tend to verify what she is saying. You simply take her as being true to her words. And you love to do so more if she is a gorgeous girl.

It was refreshing out there and the gentle air around me was filled with a wonderful blend of various scents—at times I smelled the steam of coffee, at other times I smelled the fragrance of Simar.

We sat there for a long time.

Almost an hour had passed when the bell rang again.

'It must be Tanu . . . *I will be back in 20 minutes!*' Simar said mimicking Tanu.

She was about to get up but instead I jumped out of my bean bag to answer the doorbell. It wasn't locked, though, to keep Simar comfortable. I welcomed Tanu back into my house. 'Sorry, I am late,' she apologized and walked ahead of me to look for her friend.

'Out there in the balcony,' I told her and then added, 'Watch your step!'

'What are you guys doing?' Tanu casually asked when she was able to trace Simar in the barely lit balcony.

'Ah . . . nothing much,' Simar said. I don't know, but for some reason Simar didn't have any answer to her friend's question.

'Truth or Dare,' popped out of my mouth. 'We were playing Truth or Dare.' I don't know why I said that. But I said it.

'Oh, who won?' she asked inquisitively.

Simar started giggling when she heard me cooking up this fake story for no reason.

I responded, 'No one yet, but there are strong chances that I may win.' And then I tried to change the subject. 'Sit!' I said, pushing a chair towards Tanu.

'Oh no, no. We are already late. We actually need to rush,' Tanu said instead.

'It will take me half an hour to cook. We can have dinner together,' I said. I really didn't want them to leave.

'You cook?' Tanu asked, putting her hands on her hips and giving me a surprised look.

'Yes.'

'You know how to cook?' Simar rose from her chair and joined Tanu.

I was enjoying their shock and answered as I had answered before, 'Yes,' and had the last sip of my coffee.

They were quiet for a moment.

'Why? What happened?' I asked as I got up and put the cup and cutlery in the tray, ready to take them back to the kitchen.

'Let me help you.' Simar sportingly took half of the stuff from my hands and followed me to the kitchen.

'Because we don't know how to cook! How come being a guy you know how to cook?' Tanu exclaimed from the balcony.

'There is nothing like guys can't cook and all. It is up to your need and interest. I live alone and I prefer eating Indian food and hence I cook it,' I answered. Then I asked them, 'How do you manage your meals then?'

By now Tanu too was at the kitchen door.

Simar replied, 'We eat in our mess.'

'Else we have stored surplus Maggi that we get from that Pakistani shop near the Mechelen railway station,' added Tanu.

'Oh yes, even I get Indian pulses and vegetables from that shop only,' I added.

'Simar, look at the time!' Tanu pleaded.

'Oh shit!'

'Ravin, we need to go now. We are very late.'

'Yes. And for sure we would love to eat some nice Indian food when we show up the next time!' Tanu chuckled. Simar gave her an annoyed look.

'Sure, anytime,' I responded. I knew that I wouldn't mind cooking for any of them.

At the door Tanu left first and Simar stood for a last-minute chat.

'Ah . . . thanks for coming, Simar. I really had a great time with you,' I said, before she could say anything.

'You are welcome and I must say it was a pleasant evening for me. Sorry for being late, though. Chalo, you take care now and I will leave. Happy Birthday once again!'

I smiled and waved my hand. She left. I closed my door and walked back, feeling blissful.

I felt the need to have a drink and to enjoy the last few hours of my birthday. I consumed two cans of Stellas. I emptied the second one listening to some music in my bedroom. For some unknown reason I loved boozing. Hours later my cellphone beeped. I had long been asleep then but the loud beep and vibration of the phone on my bedside woke me up. Half asleep, I read the SMS. It was her—Simar. I was drunk but tried to read the message. There were three words on the screen: 'Truth or Dare?'

It is early morning. I haven't been able to sleep much. I am out of my bed way ahead of my usual routine time. I prepare some tea for myself. Standing in the refreshing air of my cold balcony and sipping the tea from my cup, I am lost in my thoughts.

I am shuttling back and forth between my past and my present. I am trying to knit each and every vital happening from my recent life with what I have already been through in the past and am trying to infer some meaning out of it. I am not even sure if it does have any meaning.

Everything that has happened so far—my coming to Belgium, Simar's studying next to my office, our frequent interactions . . . was this all coincidence? Who was driving all this? God?

Why am I thinking about her? After all, who is she? Simply an Indian girl in Belgium, just like hundreds more. But then why am I getting so deeply attracted to her?

Wait. Am I? No, this isn't true. There is nothing of this sort. How can it be? I have already lived this phase of my life. It can't happen again.

But then there is something which is bothering me. What is it? I can lie to Sanchit but how do I lie to myself?

All of a sudden the alarm of my watch, back in my bedroom, rings at its routine time and interrupts my thoughts. I realize that I have long drunk my tea. I walk back to my room to get ready.

Eleven

That night had another surprise for me. It was long past midnight and I was wondering whether to reply to her SMS or not. The very idea of learning about each other at that hour of the night through a naughty game was really exciting me—I was on the verge of becoming crazy. I was not sure how she was feeling but the complication was also that I was high and extremely conscious of this fact. Besides, I was struggling with two types of fears at that moment—the fear of getting carried away and becoming the kind of human being I had long left behind and the fear of denying myself a chance to restart a whole new life.

Both were contradictory fears. Now that I had had my share of alcohol, the things that Sanchit had told me earlier appeared to make sense. I'd left India because I wanted a change in my life. I was in Belgium which was offering me a change. I was delighted. But I was confused too. I floated in an oblivious sea of two simple questions—should I or should I not?

I bit my lower lip, considering my next move, as if it was a game of chess and I was taking my time to play. To comfort myself, I'd bought my own argument that how could I simply go off to sleep without answering the SMS when someone, somewhere was waiting for my response. The very fact that she was waiting for me made me anxious; and I was becoming more anxious as more time passed by. I picked up my phone and willed myself to write to her that I was half asleep and would talk to her in the morning. That appeared to me as the best thing to do, especially since I wasn't sure which way I wanted my life to move.

But before I could even frame a message to send Simar, I got another one from her. It read:

'It's ok if u r scared of playing it. But u shouldn't have mentioned to Tanu that u were about to win ☺'

That smiley at the end of the message made me smile. I looked at the wall in front of me, thinking now of how to reply. That SMS was a tempting bait from a candid if not cunning mind.

Is she provoking me? I thought to myself. I couldn't sleep now! My opponent was not only beautiful but possessed smart communication skills, so smart as to entice her targets. I replied: 'Whose turn first?'

As soon as that message escaped my mobile I got a third one from her flashing on my mobile's screen.

'Ravin, I m sorry. It wasn't me. Tanu snatched my phone n sent them. Extremely sorry.'

By the time I read this, my message had already been delivered to her. Had her third message reached me two seconds back, I wouldn't have sent mine. And then another one came: 'I scolded her big time. U must hv been sleeping. Sry 2 bother u.'

To this I replied, saying: 'It's ok. Gdnite.'

A few minutes later, she responded, asking: 'U appear angry. M nt sure if u actually meant it 2 b ok. I only hope u forgive me.'

I laughed at her panic, though I was wondering why Tanu had done this.

I wrote back to her: 'Cn forgive u only on 1 condition.'

She was quick to ask: 'Wat condition?'

'Whose turn first?☺' was my condition.

By now a series of SMSs were being exchanged on our mobiles.

'U actually wana play kya?'

I loved her style of ending sentences with Hindi words.

'Hanji,' I wrote back, complementing her Hindi.

Her reply was prompt: 'Bt I ws about 2 sleep.'

To this I responded: 'Oh u need nt play it dear. Jst simply accept dat u lost n I wil frgive u n thn we both cn sleep.'

'Yaar u know I m scared of playin it. I nvr played dis game wid a guy.'

'Same pinch! Even m scared. I nvr played this wid ny gal.

U still hv Tanu 2 help u. M all alone n we r gonna play half d game. jst d truth part n nt d dare s we can't play it over the phone.'

She took her time to send her next message. I enjoyed this truce in between our war of messages.

Moments later she wrote back: 'Yeh theek rahega. But my turn first.'

'Go ahead.'

'Hmmm . . . wer u actually annoyed by d 1st msg sent by Tanu?' was her first question.

'No. In fact pass on my thnks 2 her if she is awake ☺'

'LOL!! ur turn.'

'Wer u nt afraid of sitting with me in my dark balcony?' I asked.

'Y? do u bite? ☺ well honestly, I was, bt thn u made me comfortable.'

'M glad u said tht. Ur turn.'

'Wat ws d best moment of ur bday 2day?'

'Hmm . . . best moment . . . wen u showed up.'

'Really?' she asked back.

I responded: 'Hey, u cn't ask 2 questions in one go. It's my turn now.'

She answered: '☺'

As the night progressed, so did the game of Truth or Dare. With those initial few questions and answers that we asked and answered respectively, the game had instilled an anxiety within us.

'Do u hv a gf either in Belgium or back in India?'

'No.'

'It's diff 2 accept though, yet I wil tk it assuming dat we r playing this game honestly. Ur turn.'

'I m playin it with utmost honesty. Do u hv a bf?'

'I knew u wud ask this. I had one long back. We broke up. So the answer is no.'

It had started simple and gradually turned difficult. However, the more it became difficult, the more interesting it became.

'How many euros do u earn a mnth?'

'Oh so u are jumping on to questions with numbers. U r makin it diff 4 urself!' I wrote back without answering.

'So shall I understand that u lost?' she asked back.

'4000 € a month.'

'Wow!! U r rich! Ur turn!' came her reply.

'Now dat u hv started let's cont with numbers. Wat r ur figure stats? ☺'

Few minutes passed and as I expected she slowed down.

'This is cheating!' she wrote back.

She appeared very innocent in her message. I laughed and thought of what she might be going through. I still didn't reply for some more time, trying to make her accept that she'd lost. I was still under the influence of the beer I'd had just before going to bed. I'd wanted to let myself loose.

It was 3.30 a.m. and I wondered if we were going to get any sleep at all. I picked up the cell to tell her that I was going to change the question when at that very moment her reply popped up on my screen.

'36-24-36.'

I first admired her straightforward answer and then pondered for a moment before writing my next message to her.

'Very honestly I appreciate your spirit of playing!' I wrote, as though to pat her on the back.

'Thnks. Hd u not made me comf, I wudn't hv answered this one. My turn now.'

'If dere is a gal walking in front of u, 1 who has a gorgeous figure, wch part of her body wud u most like to stare at?'

'Gorgeous figure . . . hmm . . . depends if she is walkin towards me or away frm me. Either way I wud hv sumthing to stare at.'

'That ws hell of a smart answer Ravin ☺'

The game had created a crazy but interesting atmosphere. An atmosphere of waiting for the answer while thinking of the next question. Thinking of a question which would be a little tougher to answer than the one asked before. A question that would let us fulfil the urge to knock at the doors of each other's private lives. A question which would first make you struggle to think: should I ask or should I not? Or should I frame it in better words before bombarding the opponent. I let my inner naughtiness take over.

'If I ask u 2 cum to my place rite now in watever u r wearing at this moment, so dat we sit n spend the entire night playing truth or dare in my balcony . . . wud u hv wanted 2 come?'

'I am shy!' came the response.

'That's not the answer to my question . . .' I wrote back.

It took little longer for my mobile to beep the next time. The message read: 'Yes I wud hv wanted to come bt nt wearin wat I m wearin rite now.'

I was happy to read her answer. I was glad that even though by sheer fluke I had mentioned that we were playing Truth or Dare that evening when Tanu had come to the balcony, Simar and I eventually ended up playing it.

'Btw wat r u wearin at this moment?' I wrote her back as soon as I read her message.

She was fast to reply. 'Haha. U cn't ask 2 questions in one go. It's my turn now ☺'

'Hv u evr had ny naughty fantasies for any fem who was far older thn you?'

'Yes. My computer ma'am in college ☺. My turn now . . . U can answer my previous ques!' I wrote back.

'A long white shirt till knees.'

'That's it?' I asked.

'I am honest. Btw u r again askin 2 ques in one go,' she replied.

These were just the questions to turn a girl shy but also the ones to ignite a guy's passions. It was not just the alcohol, but also the silence of the night which had turned the game sensational for both of us. That we were addicted was evident with the frequency with which we were exchanging messages. If not, then it became quite clear when I asked her:

'You want to stop the game with a draw?'

She replied: 'No! I don't mind winning or losing bt don't want 2 stop. If u wan 2 stop lemme know.'

It wasn't just a game any more. It had turned into an opportunity to discover each other. Though it had turned a bit naughty, it had still made us candid and upfront, allowing us to open up and share things. It made us comfortable and, in that short space of time, had created an intangible bond between us. I remembered the last question she'd asked.

'Now dat for the last question u hv answerd u r a virgin lemme gt bak 2 basics. Hv u evr kissed a girl?'

It was surprising for her to know that I didn't have a girlfriend and that I was a virgin. Fortunately for her and for me, I answered positive for the question on kissing a girl.

My answer gave birth to another conversation.

I was answering her confusion of me not having a girlfriend and yet kissing a girl. I told her that I was honest when I said I didn't have a girlfriend then. I did have one a few years back. She wanted to know about that girl.

I took a deep breath and wrote, 'I wud love 2 tell u about dat girl, but it is a long story and I don't want to narrate it over d phone.'

She agreed and made me promise that I would tell her the entire story by the coming weekend. I accepted her offer.

It was dawn when we finally slept. The two of us had still not called that game off. We mutually decided to continue this game till infinity, so that anytime anyone wants to ask a question, we could do so.

That game of Truth or Dare had given rise to something beautiful between us—this fact was quite apparent. For the first time in years I slept with a smile on my face.

Twelve

The next day we met for lunch. It was late in the afternoon. I had been excited the entire morning and had been looking forward to see her. When I met her, I felt that she was equally eager to see me. But there was a difference—she was mysteriously silent while I was talking a lot. I recalled the entire game we had played the night before. Many of her answers flashed in my mind. Many of my questions—which I wouldn't dare ask her to her face but had managed to do so the night before—also came to mind. I was sure she might also be feeling the same. She was the same girl who revealed '36-24-36' and I was the same guy who asked her those statistics. We both had dark circles around our eyes which were loudly advertising our lack of sleep. Though neither of us could actually go back and sleep. The sheer excitement we felt for sure wouldn't have allowed us to catch any shut-eye.

The lunch we had that afternoon was extraordinary. It was our usual tasty sandwich, the same chilly Belgian winter and the same warm sun in the sky, but for some reason they all seemed at their best that day. Needless to say, we both had been eagerly waiting for this lunch since the time we'd slept only a few hours before.

Sitting in front of Simar and watching her eat her meal, I started realizing that somewhere in the depths of my heart someone had finally broken the ice and an unidentifiable part of me had begun to melt. I felt as if it was some kind of magical metamorphosis that was happening to me. Till some time back in my life I used to be lost in my own thoughts, most of which would take me back to my past. I certainly wanted a change in my life but I was not sure how it was going to happen. I had almost believed that the rest of my life was going to continue pretty much in the same way as it had continued till then. Finding love again was not an option I ever thought of, and neither did I want to think of it. Deep in my heart I accepted that I had had my share of love in this life. So what if it had gone? At best, I used to recall my lost love and relive those memories again and again. People do live with memories—not sure how many and not sure how.

But that day onwards, I accepted that I was no longer the same Ravin I used to be. Gradually, with the passage of each day, I sensed that I was changing. I accepted that I loved Simar's company. I got all excited when I was to see her at lunch. I would feel low if she wouldn't turn up for some reason. Most of the time her name would appear on my cellphone's last dialled contact.

But despite whatever was happening to me, I must confess that there also was something that was stopping me from sailing in the oceans of my heart. Time and again a counter-thought would knock at the doors of my conscience and ask me if it was perfectly all right to allow everything to proceed the way it was happening. At times I would recall my past and try to find reasons to some unasked questions. Most of the time I wasn't sure what I was up to. But every time I was sure that I was being true to myself and to others.

Meanwhile, Simar became more comfortable with me. I remember, after that memorable lunch we had that afternoon, she said that she didn't need Tanu's company any more to visit my place. To prove her point she did turn up very quickly on my doorstep. It was the following Saturday and her second visit to my place. 'I will tell you her story,' I'd said when we had been playing Truth or Dare. And she had remembered that I had mentioned to do so over the next weekend.

This was that weekend. She settled on the couch and made herself comfortable. When I was about to get her something to drink she stopped me and said, 'I am here only to listen to your story.'

I smiled. 'So in how much detail do you want to know it?' I asked her.

'In the greatest possible detail,' she answered without taking a moment to think. Her response, however, made me thoughtful for a few moments.

'Hmmm . . .' I was looking at her.

In return she kept staring straight into my eyes, waiting for me to start narrating my story. She seemed very sure about her reason for being at my place and she didn't want to deviate from the same.

I stood for a while and then walked away. Behind me she called out, 'Where are you going?'

I ignored her and walked right to my bedroom and returned with a book—my book.

'Here is her story in the greatest possible detail,' I said as I handed that book to her.

Surprised, she quickly grabbed the book and read the title.

'I . . . too . . . had . . . a . . . love story . . .' she read and then murmured in a low voice the line below the title, 'A heartbreaking true love tale . . . Ravinder Singh.' She read my name and then reread it. And then she was left agape. She made out that it was I who had written the story when she flipped the cover page and saw my picture next to the author bio.

She didn't speak for a while, her eyes darting from the pages of the book to my face. I knew she had at least a thousand questions she wanted to ask in that one moment, but she was hardly able to frame one. And unable to do so, she sat back and tried to get a sense of it all from my book.

Even I didn't offer help with any explanations but simply stood there reading her facial expressions as she continued flipping some more pages in haste.

When she got to the summary of the book she read my tribute—'To the loving memory of the girl whom I loved, yet could not marry.' Suddenly she closed her mouth and swallowed nervously. I saw her throat muscles retract and then constrict. She seemed a little tense. Then, with a small sigh, she untied her sandals, folded her legs on the couch, leaned back and started reading the book.

I knew that with the subject of my book, the atmosphere in my living room was getting sombre. And I didn't want to make it any more emotional.

'All right, I have kept my promise. Take your time and read it at your leisure. I am going to make some tea for both of us. I want you to help me,' I said, turning towards the kitchen.

'You go and make it. I will read it now,' came a prompt answer from her.

'What?' I turned back to her.

She didn't bother to answer this time. Her eyes were glued to the book. She no longer cared to look at me. I stood there in silence for a while and left when I was sure that she wouldn't accompany me.

For the remainder of the evening she continued with her reading marathon. I wondered how she could simply sit and read without bothering about anything else. She hadn't even thanked me for the tea! I noticed that she had been quickly and continuously flipping the pages, roughly one every three minutes. Though I sat next to her and had my tea, it was as good as having it alone.

It is a rare case when a reader is so engrossed in a book that she neglects the author of the very book she is reading!

It seemed useless to sit around and wait for her to speak, so I moved to the dining table and pulled out my laptop to carry on with my office work. Some more time passed and the silence continued to prevail in the living room.

Suddenly she stood up and wore her sandals.

'What happened?' I asked, thinking that she might be wanting to use the loo.

'I have to go back. It's late!' she responded.

I looked at the wall clock. It was just 8.30 p.m. and, as such, it was not really a late hour. I knew she was used to being out of her hostel till much later in the night.

'Are you sure?'

'Yes. And I am taking this with me,' she said, looking at the book and tying the straps of her sandal with her left hand. The index finger of her right hand was wedged between the pages of the book, marking the point at which she had stopped reading.

'Have dinner, na?' I insisted.

'No . . . I need to go,' she insisted.

I got the feeling that there was something on her mind as she was behaving a little differently. But I didn't push her to stay back or to reveal what had happened to her. I let her go.

A little while later, after she had gone, she sent me a long message:

'M sry 4 leavin dis way all of a sudden. In d last chapter I witnessed u kissing Khushi n holding her in ur arms. 4 sum reasons I got conscious of lookin at u while reading about u. At dis moment m so addicted 2 ur life's story dat I don't wan 2 ruin my experience of readin it furthr n hence wanted to read it in my privacy. M in a cab n eagerly awaiting 2 rch home n continue readin it. Wll talk 2 u nxt once i complete it.'

That night there wasn't any further message from her. Neither did I write back.

Thirteen

When I woke up the next morning I realized that Simar had completed reading my book. There were a few long messages in my mobile phone that had arrived at dawn—near about 4 a.m.

The first one read: 'Jst completed readin ur life's story Ravin. I'm still crying. Last few pages of the book hv been spoiled wid patches of my tears falling on thm. Ur love 4 Khushi is so sacred n priceless. Hw cud God b so cruel 2 tk away n angel like Khushi from you? Bt u knw wat, I m happy that with this tribute to Khushi, u brought her bck in this world n defeated God. Evry girl wud yearn for a soulmate like u.'

I didn't respond to any of her messages.

Later in the day we met for lunch at the diner. She was sad and I could sense how deeply she was moved by my book. Her eyes had empathy for me. I tried to make her feel comfortable. By the time we grabbed our sandwiches and sat at the table, the two of us kept talking about Khushi. She had plenty of questions about her. To answer some of them I narrated some of the funny moments that Khushi and I shared which were not part of the book. She finally smiled and I felt a little lighter. By the time we had finished our lunch and were about to leave, she asked me the same question which millions of my readers have asked.

'Can I get to see her picture?'

I stood silently and kept looking into her eyes. Her compelling eyes had that conviction which didn't allow me to let her down. For some reason I myself wanted to show her my Khushi, even before she had asked about her. It had never happened to me this way earlier. And I believed it would never happen to me this way later.

Before the day ended I did show her what my Khushi looked like.

As Simar moved her fingers over the photograph, her only words were: 'Just the way you described her in your masterpiece.'

As the days passed by, I realized that reading my book had brought Simar far closer to me than she had ever been. It had changed a lot of things between us. It worked as a catalyst that set into motion the process of bridging the pending yet vital gaps in our budding relationship. It had made things crystal clear in Simar's mind. I could see that in her body language. I could read that in her thoughts.

Late one night, when Simar and I were talking to each other over the phone, she expressed herself clearly. She was serious about whatever she was saying.

'Having known you personally and then through your book, I wish I could have a guy like you in my life.'

I kept quiet.

'You are the sweetest heart,' she said.

'I want to hear that one more time,' I responded, having gathered my courage.

'You are *my* sweetest heart,' she said, this time with more conviction.

'I want to hear that one more time,' I hesitantly repeated. For some reason her voice was hypnotizing me.

'You are my sweetest heart, Ravin. I want to hug you.'

I kept insisting she repeat those glorious words. She kept repeating them. And the two of us kept talking late into the night. Before we had said goodnight to each other, Simar had planned to exercise her wish, to hug me, the very next day.

~

The next afternoon, I arrived at the bus stop close to my office. I had taken a half-day leave. A delighted Simar had been waiting for me. She looked refreshing in her light blue half-sleeved top. It had a witty message on the front which read 'You are wrong' in a light-coloured smaller font in the background, and 'I am right' in a larger, darker font in the foreground.

'What is with this funny message on your top—You are wrong and I am right?' I said and laughed

'Hey!' she slapped my hand as she caught me reading that on her front.

'What? Can't I read it?' I asked, smiling.

'*Har likhi hui cheez padhni zaroori nahi hoti,*' she said and took away her gaze.

'*To phir likhi kyu hoti hai?*' I asked back.

'I don't know,' she said.

I laughed and teased her further. 'Do you have a problem with me reading it or my staring at the wrong place?'

As soon as I said this her mouth opened in an oval shape, letting out a 'Haawww!' as a sign of embarrassment. Then, as if to avoid me, she looked away in the direction from which the bus was to come.

'Achha, I am sorry,' I apologized. 'But you are looking very beautiful in this top.'

Hearing this she looked back at me and couldn't help herself from smiling. I saw her twinkling eyes. She was calm yet pleasantly anxious.

My home was just a ten-minute ride away and soon we were there. As we walked from the sunlit open space into the roofed entrance of my building a chill ran into my body. I had almost started getting the vibes of what was to follow in the next few hours. We walked up to the first floor. I unlocked the door and walked in. She followed me.

As soon as I locked the door from inside, another chill ran down my spine. Not that I was scared but probably I wasn't prepared. And not that Simar was prepared, but at least she was sure of what was on her mind. And honestly, I was dependent on her. I was game for her thoughts as I had nothing to share. I had surrendered myself. What was going to happen was going to be pleasant but I wasn't sure if it was all good to let those pleasant things happen.

Simar in turn looked around. I said a few words, all of them needless. I was tracing the ground beneath my feet even though it was not a battle. She kept watching me and it was as if she was allowing me to get comfortable in my own house. I appeared almost like a loser, being in my own house and unable to cope with a situation of being with a girl who had something lovely running in her mind. My past was flashing in my mind. I had been struggling with it for so long and I was struggling with it even more so in those moments.

When the silence grew uncomfortable and I failed to find appropriate words to break it, I went to pull out a bottle of water from the fridge. The chilled air from the fridge froze me further.

'You want juice or water?' I shouted, pulling out a can of juice.

She didn't respond.

'Simar. You want—?'

I hadn't even completed my sentence when I felt Simar behind me.

She had perched her elbow on the door of the refrigerator and was watching me. She was smiling naughtily with her little fingertip stuck at the corner of her lips.

'You want a . . .' I tried to continue but she cut me in mid-sentence to say, 'I want you!'

The refrigerator door swivelled shut behind my back, interrupting my gazing at her.

The curve of her smile grew.

She didn't say anything further, but simply stepped closer towards me with her arms wide open.

In that very second I experienced a rush of adrenalin surging within me. It was as if gallons of blood were rushing up and down my nerves, choking them, and inflating my muscles inside. My hands grew cold, colder than the chilled juice cans in my hands. I put those cans on the shelf next to me, but couldn't take my eyes off her. I was a split second away from witnessing something beautiful. It wasn't going to be for the first time but it was going to be after so long a time.

She came like a breeze and wrapped me in her arms. I felt her and I felt her feeling me. She held me tight and rested her face on my left shoulder. Her warmth pushed away the cold lurking within me. Her innocent hug cleared every lingering thought from my mind, leaving me absolutely calm.

After a long time I was in a woman's arms. That one moment was as if . . . as if life had suddenly been fuelled back into me, as if it had rained again after a decade of drought . . . It felt like the first sunrise after thousands of moonless dark nights, like the first bite of bread after a hundred days of hunger.

I felt satisfied.

Tears ran down my face as I rested my face on her shoulder. She sensed that but didn't say anything; instead she gripped me tight and whispered in my ears, 'You are a sweetheart. You deserve happiness.'

I rested my head for a while on her shoulder and I gripped her tightly.

When I opened my eyes she moved her face back and looked right into my eyes. She wiped away the tears from my face. I smiled back and I hugged her again. I was happy. I don't know for how long we were there in my kitchen, holding each other in our arms, leaning against the refrigerator. I guess not until my arid heart got drenched in the shower of pleasure and warmth.

Sometimes you are not sure how happiness can again slip into your life. That was one such moment. Something within me accepted that whatever was happening was right— and for the first time I was sure of it. I felt relaxed.

We slowly moved to the living room, feeling blissful. She was smiling and touching me without feeling shy. She was sure of how she wanted to live that moment and, by then, so was I. As I sat on the couch she ran her fingers on my nose pinching the softness of my face with the tips of her nails.

Then all of a sudden she wanted to sit on my lap. I was only too eager to fulfil her wish. She kept looking at me.

'Have you ever got butterfly kissed?'

'Butterfly kissed!!' I repeated those cute words. They sounded so lovely even as I spoke them aloud.

'Hmm . . .?' She kept laughing.

'Naah . . .'

'Let me show you then,' she said as she took off her shoes and leaned over me.

'Wait! No . . . Hey, give me a moment . . .' I pleaded. I wanted to be calm enough to capture the moment to make it last longer.

But she didn't listen to me. She sealed my lips with her forefinger and pushed me back as she climbed on to me. I was still trying to speak when her body moved over my face and I reread the mantra written on her top.

You are wrong. I am right.

I simply smiled and politely surrendered myself to her.

She rolled up and down over me to find the right posture after which she executed her butterfly kiss.

She confidently blew a puff of air on to my eyes and brought her right eye close to my right eye. I was about to close my eyes when she whispered not to do so in my ear. Her hair smelled amazing. I felt her poised body on me. It was great to hold her. She then beautifully fluttered her eyelashes against mine. I followed her in doing the same. The tiny hairs of our eyelashes rubbed against each other, fluttering like butterflies in harmony.

'You know what you are now experiencing?' she asked passionately and politely.

'A butterfly kiss!' I answered.

A little later, she slid down and connected her lips with mine. I firmly held her in my arms and turned her over so that I could be on top of her. She allowed me to. Then I gently took her lower lip within mine and watched her closing her eyes. I kissed her passionately.

We remained on that couch for a long time.

~

Almost two hours after having an incredible time, Simar and I were outside her institution. Simar was set to go on a weekend trip with her college friends. It was more of a formal college trip else she would have cancelled it. None of us wanted to part ways. And this fact was visible on her innocent face.

'Can I fall sick and stay back?' she asked me, cutely pouting her lips like a kid and as usual letting her head bend sideways.

'No, dear,' I said and rubbed her cheek with my hands. I didn't want her to suddenly change her focus from her college to me.

We were still standing there, talking, when Tanu gave her a call on her mobile phone. Simar turned to leave when I pulled out that juice can which I had picked up for her before leaving from my home. Back at my place we had been so busy that we didn't have time for anything else. She was overjoyed when I gave the can to her. She felt I cared. I planted a kiss on her forehead and waved goodbye. She left for her trip. I left for my office.

We kept exchanging warm SMSs over the phone till late at night. I was very tired, yet I forced my eyes open to read and reply. The anticipation of waiting to receive her next message was tickling me inside. And every time my cellphone vibrated it made my heart pleasantly skip a beat. A bit of anxiety, a bit of fresh romance and a bit of drowsiness had all effectively intoxicated me till sleep overtook my senses.

I am at some place. I don't know exactly where. It's a strange place. It is all bright around me. A pin-drop silence persists; like the silence of the dawn before the sunrise. I feel very light as I walk on the path in front of me. I don't know why I am here or where I need to go. Yet I am walking. Though I have never been here before, I can feel a strong connection with this place . . . That scent! I know that scent!

All of a sudden I see someone in front of me. A girl! She is facing away from me. As I walk towards her the intensity of her perfume increases. I am a few steps away from her now. I hear someone's heartbeat. I am standing behind her and about to see her but before I can see her, she utters, 'Shona!'

And then she turns around to face me and leaves me in a shock. It's her. It's Khushi.

A cool breeze blows and everything around me glitters. I see her and she looks at me. All of a sudden I don't sense the ground beneath me. I am floating in the air. I am glued to her and not a single muscle in me moves.

She keeps staring at me for long and we talk through our eyes. She speaks. I listen.

She then rubs her hand on my cheek and says, 'I am happy for you!' And she smiles.

I still can't move but a tear from the corner of my right eye rolls down, on to her hand. I want to speak but can't.

The light around both of us brightens up every second. It blurs my eyes. And all of sudden the intensity of the brightness blinds me in a flash.

She vanishes.

Fourteen

Soon it was Simar's birthday. I woke up early and, after getting dressed, I went to a florist. Unlike India, in the West we don't find roadside florists which open that early in the morning. Like a crazy lover I roamed outside the Carrefour mall, waiting for it to open its doors. Thankfully for me, it opened sharp at 8 a.m. I was the only shopper in the thousand-yard store!

'*Bonjour, monsieur!* (Hello, sir!)' the lady at the billing counter wished me.

'*Bonjour!*' I wished her back. '*Pour cinq euros?* (For five euros?)' I asked her in my broken French, showing the bouquet of red and white roses that I had picked.

'*Sûr oui* (Sure, yes),' she said.

'Ah! Pack this, *sil vous plait* (please),' I said to her in a hurry, writing a birthday note for Simar. '*Merci!* (Thank you!)' I said and ran out as soon as I got the bouquet.

I caught my bus from a different stop and followed an extended route to drop by her hostel. It was 8.30 when I reached her hostel. I called her on the cellphone.

She picked up the phone and said 'hello'.

I didn't say anything but began to whistle the Happy Birthday tune.

On the other side I could hear her giggling and then laughing alternately.

'Happy Birthday, sweetheart!' I finally whispered into the phone

'Thank you, Ravz!' she said. She was still laughing. 'It's so sweet of you!'

She had plenty of nicknames for me. From my already bonsai name of Ravin she managed to shorten it further to Ravz. But it did not stop there. She would often distort it further at her will—it mostly depended on her mood. The most common nicknames she came up with were Ravzu or Ravzi. And at times she would stretch it to Ravzzi-i-i-i-i-i-i' when she wanted to sound extra cute so that I would complete her assignments for her. The shortest one was simply Ro. I didn't like the last one. For some reason it made me feel like a pet. When I told her what I felt about it, she stopped using it.

'Now will you come down or should I barge into the girls' hostel?' I asked.

'Oh, are you outside? Here?' she asked excitedly.

'Yes, baby!' I said.

Minutes later I saw her running out of her building. She was in her nightdress and her hair was not made; her face wasn't as fresh as I had seen it earlier. But she looked cuter than she had looked before. It's good to see beauty in its purity, untouched.

She was smiling. I knew she had not brushed yet but her teeth were shining white—a trait I'd most admired in her and also told her about.

As she came closer to me, I pulled out the bouquet from my bag and presented her.

'Happy Birthday once again!'

I hugged her and kissed her cheek. She looked at the bouquet for a while and looked back at me, still smiling.

'There is a note in it,' I said.

'*Oh haan! Ravz, ismein to kuch likha hua hai!*' she exclaimed, her eyes twinkling with anticipation. She took her sweet time in reading the note, standing a foot away from me to read peacefully. She stood in her favourite posture—legs straight and head tilted over her left shoulder.

I wrote a few lines about her to make her feel good.

When she had finished reading, she rushed to me with open arms and hugged me tightly.

'Thank you so much, Ravz. You remembered my birthday and you made it so special for me,' she said smiling. We talked for a while and walked in the garden area of her hostel after which I left for my office.

On my way to office I messaged her: 'U shd now read what's on the back of the note.'

In the next minute she replied: 'Oh! *Ye to aur ek surprise nikla Ravz.* Love u! I will be ready.'

The back of the note read: We are going for dinner tonight. Be ready at 8. I know you don't have any evening lectures today. Don't ask me how I managed to know that.

~

It was late in the evening and I had managed to get Anthony's car.

Although Anthony was part of my client's team, he was more of a friend to me—though still not good enough a friend to let me borrow his Volkswagen for an evening.

I had won his car for that evening in a bet.

The previous evening Anthony and I had left the office a little early. We played a best-of-five series in pool. The bet was that if I lost I would gift him the best red wine in this country and if he lost, he would let me borrow his Volkswagen for one evening. I had cleverly laid out the terms before the beginning of the game.

'You sure you won't step back if you lose? It's 200-plus euros—the red wine I am talking about. I hope you know that?' Anthony had said confidently.

Anthony was a great player and I had known his skills in pool from the past game he had won against me. But I also knew that despite always playing a straight forward game against him without devising any strategy, I had still given him tough competition. I made him accept my challenge. The bet I'd proposed for him was quite big.

The series ran not just till the fifth rack but with the final black ball on the table—the last ball to be potted in the game of pool. Whosoever pots it turns out to be the winner.

That was the level of the game. We literally battled on the table of pool—one for the charm of wine and the other for the charm a woman. And none of us wanted to invest our own wealth to win these charms. By the way that reminds me of the third 'W' that I keep forgetting: 'Wealth, women and wine can make anything happen in this world!'

In the end Anthony potted the black ball.

The irony was that he potted it in the wrong pocket and thus lost the series to me. I was on cloud nine!

Anthony kept his promise.

And finally I was there outside Simar's hostel—in the Volkswagen, of course. Simar came out and, not able to see me, dialled my number.

'Where are you?'

'Very close to you.'

'But I don't see you.' And she looked here and there.

'You are almost looking at me,' I said, artfully indicating that she should keep looking straight ahead. Her mouth opened in astonishment as I rolled down the windowpane. She stood there with her mouth open for twenty-odd seconds.

I came out of the car. 'Run!' I shouted, calling her towards me.

She willingly obliged.

We hugged again and, looking quite pleasantly surprised, she asked, 'Whose car is this?'

'First sit inside, then I will tell you,' I said.

She was happy. And I was happy that she was happy.

Moments later, I was telling her how I had got the car for her. She put her head on my shoulder and enjoyed listening to my story.

We spent the first half of the evening buying gifts for her. I wanted to gift her nice formals which she could wear during her placement season. We tried various shops but liked nothing. Actually, I liked a few but she didn't. Sometimes it was the design, sometimes the colour and if both were perfect then the cloth wasn't perfect. Girls have this tendency to not like anything in the first phase of shopping. Basically, they want to consider everything first and then make their decision.

So finally we were in the second half of our buying session. My girlfriend was in the changing room and had been constantly shouting from inside, asking me to either bring a different size or a different colour of the dresses she had been trying on. Every time she would ask for something she would throw a dress over the door. It was like playing badminton with the dresses! Also, she wouldn't tell me whether she would be throwing her top or skirt out. I had to be alert all the time and when I wasn't it would land squarely on my head or shoulders!

But I was game for it all. I had taken it for granted that I was at her command for this time period. It was funny, though, to constantly walk into the women's section, take the help of a lady assistant to find out a different size or a different colour of that dress and walk back to deliver it to Simar. It turned embarrassing when I repeated this exercise some twenty-odd times—even more so each time I passed the deadly lingerie section full of seductive stuff. I only thanked my stars that Simar wasn't trying any of them on. I was even scared to imagine myself carrying lingerie of different colours and sizes for her. The salesgirls noticed me smiling. Back in their heads they were probably asking: are you actually going to buy any?

At times, when Simar liked something, she was kind enough to open the door and show me. One time she opened the door and then laughed when she saw me. I had a dozen ladies' dresses hanging on both my shoulders. I looked more like a salesman for ladies garments!

'Oh, this one looks perfect on you!' I had started saying that to everything that she wore to help her decide quickly.

In the end, instead of formals, we ended up buying casuals for her, just because of the 'Oh boy!' factor the moment she put them on. It was a polo-necked, full-sleeved top with horizontal lines of light blue and grey along with grey denims which had a girlish glittering print on the back pockets. She actually looked perfect! I was awestruck watching her in them. She loved flaunting them too and kept posing in front of the giant mirrors—even the ones which were outside the changing room.

I was conscious of the way she was showing off in public. But nothing seemed to bother her. However, she seemed totally unaware of people around her. She was busy twirling in front of the mirrors, watching how her body looked from every angle in her new apparel.

Once I paid for the dress we were back in the car.

'You almost forgot me, buying these clothes,' I said, trying to tell her how she was obsessed with the clothes and assumed that I was at her beck and call.

'How can I forget you, baby?' she asked seductively, coming closer to me, pulling my cheeks and kissing me.

I was pleased that she loved what we bought.

I looked at her as I drove. She looked at me, winked and smiled. Her hands were now playing with my hair. Then she kissed me again. Suddenly I applied the brakes of the car.

'What happened?' she asked.

I didn't reply but held her face in my hands and took her lips in mine. It happened on the spur of the moment. She responded with fierce passion. She pulled my upper lip in her mouth while her hands rubbed my back passionately. The taste of her mouth lingered on my lips. I undid my seat belt and leaned over her. We stared at each other, our lips open and throbbing with desire. She looked into my eyes. We began to kiss passionately gain. I held the nape of her neck and kissed her all the way down her cleavage before my lips made their way back to her chin.

'Kiss me harder,' she whispered.

The sounds of our kissing echoed within that silent and intense atmosphere inside the car. We could feel and hear each other's breath. Soon our kisses became longer and more ardent. It went on as if it would never end. Our lips and tongues were locked with each other's. We continued our passionate smooching in Anthony's Volkswagen for a long while.

Much longer than the time Simar spent in finalizing which clothes to buy.

~

Later that evening Simar and I went to an Indian restaurant. We had a lavish candlelit dinner. In the light of the candle between us, all I could see was her perfectly beautiful face. Seeing her then I also recalled how she had appeared to me that morning, moments after she had gotten up from her bed, when I had brought her the flowers. And while we ate to our hearts' content, we talked at length about our respective families back in India, our past and our good friends.

We continued to talk on the same subject as I drove Simar back to her hostel. It was 11.30 p.m. by then. Her hostel was some 500 metres ahead when I stopped the car. It was a dark and abandoned part of the street. There was a kennel just nearby and I parked the vehicle in the open ground in front of the kennel. Up above, the half-moon in the sky was playing hide-and-seek behind the clouds. She wondered why I'd stopped the car. For a moment I didn't speak. She waited for me to speak. I raised my chin and looked at her.

'I wanted to gift you something else on your birthday,' I said huskily.

She smiled and then said, with wonderment in her eyes, 'What? . . . I already have my gifts on the back seat.'

'Not the materialistic ones,' I answered.

'Okay,' she said and crossed her arms across her chest and turned towards me, giving me all her attention. There was pin-drop silence around us.

'You will find it stupid, but I wrote a few lines for you.'

'Oh wow, Ravz! Really? Will you sing them for me?' she said. I nodded. Biting her lower lip, she waited for me to start, her eyes twinkling with love as they focused on mine.

I smiled back and rolled my eyes, acknowledging her.

She clapped and then waited. I began singing.

'*Hmmm . . . jaana suno . . .*'

I looked at her and paused. I thought it wasn't going well and I was shy.

'Sing, na, Ravz! I am dying to listen to it.

'*Jaana suno, kuch to kaho, hamse yu naa tum rutha karo . . .*'

As I sang for her I don't know how or why it happened but the dogs from the kennel above started howling. I don't know if they were crying or singing with me.

Simar and I looked at each other and then for a minute listened to the howling of the dogs and broke into a laugh. Nothing seemed to matter—we rather enjoyed it.

'Ravz, continue, na. Let them give the background music.'
And she kept her eyes glued to me.

'I wrote this one when we fought the other day and you
were not talking to me,' I said, telling her the inside story.

She nodded her head in acknowledgement and waited for
me to resume my singing.

Jaana suno, kuch to kaho, hamse yu naa tum rutha karo.
Apna to saath kuch aisa, jaisa chaand ka sitaaro se ho.
Hmmm . . . Jaana suno, sunti raho, hamse yu naa tum rutha karo.
Apna to saath kuch aisa, jaisa nadiya ka kinaaro se ho
Hmmm . . . laaa laaa la laa, laaa laaa la laaa . . .'

I stopped. But, surprisingly, the dogs continued.

Simar kept looking at me.

'*Bas itna hi tha,*' I said smiling.

She didn't laugh. She came closer to me and held my face
in her hands. I could see her eyes were wet.

She kissed my forehead.

The dogs continued their cacophony in the background.

'There is something that is left,' I said.

She wasn't in a state to talk and could only raise her chin
in question. I could see that she could no longer control her
tears which were now making their own way down her
cheeks. I watched her in silence and even allowed her to
cry. She probably wanted to say sorry for the other day but
wasn't able to express her apology. Her tears seemed to
transform into vapours of divine happiness somewhere in
the air between her and me.

I went ahead to say, 'You have given a new life to me. I had been in love in the past. This now seems like déjà vu. I don't know how this is happening. I don't know if this is the right thing to happen or not. But I am sure this is happening . . . Looking back at my life, I realize that I had accepted the fact that I could cherish my share of love only in the memories from my past. I never wanted to lose those memories and I still don't want to lose them. This is the very reason I thought I could never and I would never be in love again. But it's all different now. On the one hand, I am still holding those memories close to my heart and willing to accept that it was my past; and on the other hand, I am willing to shape up my future. And to shape up my future it is not essential that I forget my past. Memories will still be there. Things are changing now. Yes, they are. Honestly, I didn't yearn for this metamorphosis. But now that it is happening, I am finding myself slipping into this pool of love again. In the initial days I couldn't believe it. I have struggled with myself to believe it, to feel it, to accept it, to digest it and finally live it. But now that I am so sure I want to say this to you . . .' I paused before continuing again, '. . . I am in love with you. Yes, I am. And I am so sure about it that I want to propose to you . . . Will you be mine?'

She continued looking at me with rapt attention. Her eyelashes were still damp. She nodded her head slightly, showing her acceptance, and closed her eyes. Her body language seemed to say that she too was sure of what she was promising and that she didn't need to think about something so obvious. In a sudden gush of tears she hugged me. We held each other in that magical space filled with those vapours of divine happiness and we now breathed in that magical air.

'I will be,' she whispered in my ears.

I kept hugging her for a while.

Some more time had passed—I don't know how much, but the dogs were quiet now.

She said it was the best birthday she'd ever had. We drove back.

Story of the fight we had the other day:

'Ravz, cancel it then. I don't care!' Simar says, sitting with one leg draped over the other, her right foot suspended above the ground and shaking purposefully. Every time she sits like this, she keeps shaking her free foot. With her arms across her chest she continues to look away from me. She is furious.

We had planned an outing for this evening but all of a sudden I have this urgent conference call with my offshore team at the same time.

'Why would you care, baby? It is my meeting, na? And I'll be held responsible for not conducting it.' Saying this, I smile. And I continue to look at her.

I had just supplied fuel and oxygen to the fire in my room.

'Ravz, don't you dare laugh, okay!' She turns and looks at me only to scare me with her big eyes and her raised finger.

Once a month, only for a few days, my charming sweetheart transforms into a furious avatar. Biology offers a decent biological name for these days—menstrual days. I had my own dictionary term for it—my hopeless days!

She would be irritated with every little thing. Every action–reaction of mine would go for a toss. Logic, rationale and, most importantly, common sense will, all of a sudden, fail to exist. Mood swings drive everything. And I, an author of a national bestseller, would go from being her boyfriend to becoming her puppy at her command.

And it wasn't only limited to handling her tantrums. I had gone as far as standing in the women's section of the chemist shop, trying to hide my embarrassment and gather my strength, all at the same time, before having to speak up and announce what I was looking for.

More than becoming her monthly problem, it all had become my monthly problem.

I attend my conference call. We don't go on the planned outing. Back at her place she is sad and isn't talking to me. Alone in my home I am being creative working on a jingle to please her: 'Jaana suno, kuch to kaho, hamse yu naa tum rutha karo!'

Fifteen

Anthony had to go to Germany to handle a field installation of our product. He called me in the morning to update me on this unplanned trip and, more importantly, to inform me that his Volkswagen would be in my custody for another day till he returned.

'Love you, Anthony. And you better work hard!' I teased him over the phone.

'Bastard!' he yelled at me and then laughingly said, 'Take care of it more than you take care of your girl.'

I utilized this opportunity to the fullest. Instead of catching my bus I drove the car to the office. I consciously matched my timing with that of the bus so that I could overtake it and show off to the others travelling in the bus to their respective offices.

His car had the inbuilt function of linking my cellphone, through Bluetooth, with the car's speakers and the overhead installed microphone. I had heard Anthony taking calls by using the controls on his steering wheel. With that system one doesn't even need to wear a hands-free. On one occasion Anthony had taken his wife's call who wasn't aware that I was sitting next to Anthony. She kissed into the phone so noisily that it echoed in the car's woofers. Anthony had been embarrassed.

I synchronized my mobile with the car's system and then I dialled Sanchit's number.

'Hey, are you guys in the 9.10 a.m. bus?'

'Yes. Why didn't you show up today?'

'Look to your right.'

Sanchit, who was at the third window seat from the front, turned to look out. He smiled first and then waved at me. Others followed. I waved at them back. For a short while I was a hero.

'*Kiski churai hai?*' Rishab grabbed Sanchit's phone to talk to me.

'*Anthony ki.*'

'*Vo jiske saath tu pool khelta hai?*'

'*Haan.*'

'*Raat ko ghumne ka plan banaatey hai phir. Bol, chalega?*'

'*Chalunga, but Simar ke saath . . . Hahahaha . . .*'

Rishab cursed me before putting the phone down.

I waved goodbye, pushed the accelerator and overtook the bus.

In the evening I left the office early to pick Simar up. I had already spoken to her about our plans in the evening.

I met her at the gate of her hostel. She was wearing a purple dress. It had a thin lacy strap running across her shoulders. The shades of purple got a little darker just above her knee where that dress ended. Her legs were smooth, long and attractive. She was wearing a pair of silver stilettos to match her dress.

We drove out of the city towards the east. It took us fifteen minutes to get on to the highway. Simar connected her little light blue iPod Nano to the music system of the car and some peppy numbers came on. The ride had just turned amazing. The weather that day was awesome. We drove by the countryside. On our way we passed various big and small hamlets. Every other house had a lush green courtyard. Some among them had their domestic animals harnessed under bamboo shelters. Simar got very excited when she saw a few white horses with styled hair at their hooves. They appeared like a royal species.

The highway lanes were wide and there was almost no traffic. After every five to eight miles we would find a gas station. From a distance, we noticed one which also had a coffee shop symbol on its billboard. We stopped there.

We loaded the vehicle with gas and got ourselves some coffee. Then we came out and stood near our car. The miles and miles that stretched before us were all green. Just about two or three trucks in the far distance made up our vision of the road ahead. The limited number of people we could see were at the gas station itself.

Simar and I walked to the front of the car and perched on the bonnet with steaming cappuccinos in our hands. It was quite pleasant to be in the countryside. The sun hung low in the western skies. The birds chirping high above our heads were probably returning to their nests. It was a beautiful evening. The countryside air smelled nice and refreshing. There was greenery all around us. The tall trees stood firm on both sides of the highway. They looked old, probably more than hundred or even two hundred years. It was different and amusing for us to not talk but simply enjoy being in that moment.

A cool breeze kept entertaining us. Time and again strands of Simar's hair would fall over her face and she would keep moving them back. One moment, while she was sipping coffee, I moved the strands of her hair behind her ear, and the touch of my finger behind her ear seemed to arouse her. She kept looking at me with expectation. I too looked deep into her eyes, which seemed to suddenly pull me towards them. I looked at her for a few seconds. Then, when I couldn't resist myself, I brought my face closer to hers and tasted her cappuccino-coated lips. That tasted far better than my own cappuccino. Simar held my face in her palms and kissed me harder. We didn't have to worry about kissing each other in the open. It is quite common to express your love this way not only in Belgium but in other parts of the West too. I love Belgium for its openness. We were still on the bonnet of Anthony's Volkswagen and it made a creaky sound under our weight as we got busy in shuffling our positions while kissing each other. Suddenly I recalled Anthony's last instructions on the phone—*Take care of it more than you take care of your girl*—and I withdrew.

Soon the weather got windy and black clouds hovered on the Belgian sky. Simar locked both her arms across my left arm and paddled her legs in the air. She said something. When I looked at her, she laughed. She had remembered a few words from the song I recited to her the night before. '*Jaana suno* . . . La la laaaa la laa . . . Hahaha,' she laughed then and said, '*Ravz, kitne funny ho tum, yaar.*' And then she laughed again. It was lovely to see her so carefree and joyful.

Then it started drizzling and we rushed inside the car. All of a sudden we inhaled the fresh revitalizing scent of the wet soil. I ignited the engine and we drove back to the city. Everything around us was breathtaking—the rain, the wind and the greenery outside the car and the melodious music, the hot cappuccino and my beautiful Simar inside the car. Each time the car's wiper would mop the windscreen, sending splashes of rainwater off the side, everything in front of us would appear clean and clear for a split second and then it would all get blurred yet again. It was going to be one of the most memorable evenings.

After a drive of fifty-odd kilometres we were back at my place. It was still raining and Simar opted to stay back. We were hungry. We stretched out for some time on the living-room couch before getting up to prepare dinner for ourselves.

We cooked jeera rice and some egg curry. Simar cut some salad and arranged the table. To celebrate the evening further we had picked up a bottle of champagne on our way back. For Simar, who had never boozed, we had bought the champagne which barely had any alcohol content. I got the bottle while Simar brought out the cutlery and the food to the table. We switched off all the lights, apart from the one which hung over the dining table, illuminating only the table area. I popped open the champagne and the frothy drink gushed out of the bottle. I served it in two glasses and handed one to Simar. We raised a toast to the beautiful evening. Under the warm light it was just the two of us. We kept talking to each other as we ate dinner. The hot steam rising from the rice gently fogged our vision, adding to the romance of the night. It also made us feel pleasantly warm. Outside, the rain had turned everything cold. As Simar and I drank and ate we recalled how we'd met for the first time at the gym, what we then thought of each other and where finally our destinies had brought us.

It was the first night that Simar was going to spend with me. An hour later, I was holding her, and my hand was firmly clasping her back. We were in the balcony; the same place where Simar and I sat for long when she had first come on my birthday. It was still dimly lit and we enjoyed the sound of the rain and the gusts of chilly air. She leaned her back against my chest; I wrapped my arms around her from behind, placing my hands on her stomach and resting my chin over her right shoulder. We stood in that warm cuddle, staring into the distance. She felt warm, she said. I naughtily moved my finger over her dress on her stomach and discovered her belly button. She giggled when I circled the tip of my finger in the depth of her naval. It tickled her.

She whispered, 'Stop doing that. I feel butterflies in my stomach.'

Late in the night the two of us made love in my bedroom. Outside it continued to rain. That was the first time we fully discovered each other. I kissed her everywhere as I explored each beautiful part of her. I knew she enjoyed my doing so, and so did I.

It was certainly the most romantic day of our lives.

'I will never forget this evening,' she said as we lay together, saturated by our love.

'I am glad we are together,' I said.

By the time we slept it was quite late at night. The rain had finally stopped.

Sixteen

It was mid-July. Summer was at its peak.

During this time of the year the days in western Europe are long enough and have sunlight beyond 9 or at times even 9.30 in the night. Belgian evenings therefore tend to be longer. On those evenings, Simar and I used to spend more time at the gym.

Once, when we met late after sundown, Simar shared a secret wish of hers. She wanted to booze. I was pleasantly surprised. She had mentioned that she had never had a drink before, apart from the champagne the other night—which contained very little alcohol content—nor did she have any plans to do so.

'How come you have this urge all of a sudden?' I questioned her.

'Just like that,' she answered candidly. I kept looking at her thinking that she would say something more as an explanation. But she didn't. That was it.

'Big deal!' she said, showing off and then giggling.

I rechecked, 'Are you sure?'

She nodded and then anxiously awaited my response. It was strange but I was enjoying this sudden urge of hers to do something crazy.

'Do you think it is a bad idea?' she asked innocently. Her eyes seemed to want me to say it wasn't.

I simply followed her eyes.

In a short while we were at a nearby Chinese restaurant. Both of us loved Chinese food and we had identified a few good Chinese eating joints in the city. We took the corner table with a sofa which Simar chose for us. We sat right beside the bar. This would not only be extremely convenient but would also give us some much-needed privacy.

The waiter handed the menu to Simar and I kept watching her take a decision on what she would drink. Her choice of booze was dependent on how nice the bottle at the bar looked and not on its contents. So she spent her time going through the deck of bottles at the bar. I enjoyed seeing her immature decision-making capabilities on the subject of alcohol. She spent some ten minutes surveying the bottles, only to come back confused to me.

'Ravz, every bottle looks amazing. Which one should we have?'

In certain moments when Simar would talk in this ultra-cute manner, I would refrain from answering immediately. I rather wanted to keep observing the little kid in my grown-up girl. I wanted to cherish the cuteness with which she talked. I wanted to share a part of her innocence and read those little things running in her sharp mind. I wanted to observe her eyes, the way they restlessly shifted between me and the bottles. I wanted to observe her lips, how they curved when she smiled, how she bit the lower one. I wanted to focus on how she wrinkled her nose when she was disappointed in one of the bottles. How her eyelashes would flutter and kiss each other for a split second after every few seconds. I wanted to just absorb each and every tiny movement on her face and in her body language. And whenever I got to live such moments, I simply wanted to keep looking at her and fulfil my lust of seeing her for an infinite duration. I wanted to become a silent observer. I never wanted to talk.

But whenever I did that, she would become shy and insist that I take my gaze off her which I would do reluctantly.

It was going to be Simar's first encounter with alcohol and, on my suggestion, she opted for a beer. I gave her two reasons: one, that among all the drinks this contained the least amount of alcohol; two, that Belgium was known for its beer. She brushed aside my first suggestion. Her plan was to get drunk with something that tasted good too, so she wasn't really worried about the level of alcohol. Luckily for me, my second suggestion appealed to her.

Since the time we had ordered the drinks, she had this anxiety and excitement to have the first sip. I could see that excitement in the mischievous glint in her eyes and also sense it in her questions, all of which were on the bar and the bottles beside us.

The waiter served the drinks along with the snacks we had ordered. Simar was moments away from taking the first sip of Belgium's renowned alcoholic drink. That's how she wanted to remember it. I gave her a little tip on how to say cheers and to keep the glass back on the table after the first sip. She went ahead and followed my instructions completely, barely containing her excitement.

But as soon as she tasted it, her euphoria drooped. Acting brave, she didn't say much—but the way her eyes shut tightly the moment she sipped the beer revealed the reality. It hadn't tasted as per her expectations. On her lips was a white moustache of froth.

'So, how is it?' I asked, smiling, and wondered what she would say.

'I knew it was going to taste bad. But I had been told by friends that this is how alcohol is supposed to be,' she answered.

I liked her spirit.

'Go slow and complement every sip with some snacks. It will help you,' I answered protectively.

In the initial few sips, Simar did struggle with the taste. It seemed it was an effort for her to swallow the spirit down her throat. But as the evening moved on, Simar did give her best shot to understand, accept and adapt to the taste of booze.

We kept talking about ourselves and the people in the restaurant. We talked about the taste of the snacks and beer. Most of the time, I kept giving her my share of gyaan on alcohol. Even though I wasn't much of a drinker, I still had the experience of drinking.

Soon there came a time when alcohol took effect. It had tickled the pleasure cells in her brain. That's when taste didn't matter any more. We continued to eat and drink, and we talked a lot. We talked crazy. Actually, it was Simar who was talking crazy. I was just acknowledging her chatter in the same tone. I was enjoying being with her. I was enjoying seeing this totally different side to her. She was enjoying making the best out of the bitter-tasting beer. She let herself go, enjoying her high because she knew that I was with her. She had said she was comfortable with me.

But all of a sudden I was beginning to think about my comfort level. My girlfriend was pitch drunk with only a pint of beer and had starting singing songs.

Hindi songs! In a Chinese restaurant! Amidst a Belgian crowd!

I wanted her to enjoy herself, though certainly not at the cost of being a public embarrassment. But she was unstoppable. Fortunately, there were not many people occupying the immediate tables beside us and thankfully she wasn't loud enough for others who sat at tables further away. She picked one line and tested my nerves by singing it I don't know how many times!

'*Aaja-aaja-neeley* la-la-la-la-la-la-laaaaaa—*JAI HO!*'

And every time, exactly two seconds later, she would add another '*JAI HO*', the only clearly audible part of her song.

I tried my best to control her but I couldn't help myself from laughing when she asked, 'Ravz, you don't like A.R. Rahman, kya?'

She was completely drunk by now and I realized the change in her body language.

Seeing the squad of bartenders and waiters observing us I was a little alarmed and began to insist that Simar behave herself. She gave me a look as if I had denied her her moral right. I quickly called on the waiter to get the menu card to order the main course.

As the waiter arrived at our table, Simar tried reading the name tag right above the pocket of his tuxedo. She actually got close enough to him while reading it.

'Lee . . .' she said first and then continued to add, 'Chang . . .' She was about to spell the remaining two letters of one of the most difficult names she had encountered in her life, when I cut her short.

'Simar!'

'Yes,' she said and shifted her focus back to me. She was smiling all the time.

'Excuse me.' I begged pardon from the waiter for Simar's behaviour. Then I asked Simar what she would prefer for dinner. She looked here and there wondering what she wanted next that evening.

'What are those people having along with lemon in those tiny glasses?' she asked me, pointing to a bunch of people at the bar.

I looked behind.

'That's tequila,' I answered and continued asking her about what she wanted to eat.

But she ignored me completely and screamed, 'Oh! Tequila shots!!'

She had added her knowledge to the little amount of information I had provided and was feeling on top of the world. I knew she was not going to give any suggestions on the food.

I looked at the menu and ordered some fried rice and seasonal vegetables dipped in garlic sauce. The waiter left the table and I found that Simar was still waiting for me to acknowledge her previous suggestion.

'Yes, they are tequila shots.'

She clapped her hands and demanded, 'I want to have those shots!'

She was already one drink down and in the middle of her second glass of beer.

'No, dear,' I persuaded her. 'This is the last one and you shouldn't mix two different drinks.'

On the one hand, I smiled at her as I told her to take it easy while on the other hand, I was worried about the reaction of the people in the restaurant. I tried my best to explain to her that we were in a public place and we should maintain decorum.

Without saying a single word she nodded. It was a big enough nod that her head tilted all the way back and then came down; three times in sequence, after which she pulled up her feet on to the sofa and relaxed. I somehow managed to control my laughter and struggled with two different thoughts.

In that very moment she was provoking me to love her and in that same moment she was pissing me off.

'Simar, take your feet off the sofa and sit properly!' I almost shouted at her.

'Shhhhhhh!!!!' she hushed with a finger on her tightly closed lips. 'We are in a public place, Ravin. Don't shout.' And she closed her eyes and relaxed for a while. She was thoroughly enjoying the essence of her drink.

This was enough time for me to take her glass back. She revolted. I still managed to take it away. Then for a while I kept her involved in conversation. I wanted to divert her attention, so that she would get a little serious. I talked to her about her MBA programme. She didn't get into the details and ended up saying that all was going well. I talked about her friends and she said they were all nice human beings. Under the influence of alcohol, she only had such positive answers to all my questions.

I was in the middle of talking to her when all of a sudden one blunder occurred. She got a call on her mobile. It was from her mother.

She showed me her mobile and all I could say was, 'Shit!'

Simar was not in a condition to talk to her mother. For her mother, I was sure, didn't think that Simar could ever dare to booze.

I was watching Simar. It seemed as if a part of her brain was alert to the upcoming danger, while another part had failed to realize what was happening.

As the phone continued to ring, pressure mounted in my brain. Simar in one instance was worried and in the other instance laughed at my panic. In her drunken state of mind she had somehow mistaken her mother to be my mother. So she started laughing, wondering how I would talk to my mom while I was drunk. I had a feeling that by now the bartenders who were watching us carefully were thinking that we had actually gone nuts. In panic I quickly looked carefully for the button to turn her phone silent. One full ring and we didn't pick up the call. The very next moment it rang again. I told Simar to sit calmly and to not go anywhere. Then I went out to the gallery and disconnected the call. I then quickly jotted down her mom's cell number and switched off Simar's phone. I had a plan in my mind.

I called up her mom from my cellphone. I had already spoken to Aunty in the past when Simar had introduced me to her. That actually worked in my favour.

'Hello Aunty!' I said.

'Hello Ravin. How are you?' she asked.

'I am good, Aunty. Aaa . . . uh . . . Simar called me up just now from her friend's cellphone,' I continued, desperately trying to cook up a story.

'Yes,' she answered. 'I was trying her just now but for some reason she didn't pick up her call?' She appeared curious.

'Yes, yes, Aunty, that's why she called me. Her phone was low on battery and as soon as she picked up your call it switched off. She is out at a party with her college friends and she told me that she will call you tomorrow morning,' I lied.

'Oh, okay . . . Yes, it rang twice but then when I tried again I got to know that her phone is switched off.'

'Yes, Aunty, that's why she called me from her friend's mobile.'

'That's okay, beta. How are you otherwise?' she checked.

I breathed a sigh of relief and went on lying some more. 'I am good, Aunty. I have a conference call with my India office people so I need to rush.' In truth, I wanted to rush back and check on Simar.

In this world where it is difficult to handle one woman, I was handling two at the same time. Worse still, it was a mother–daughter combo!

As soon as I had finished the call I ran back to the dining hall where I soon realized that my troubles were not yet over. Simar was missing from her seat. She was at the bar!

Two little empty glasses of tequilas were rolling on the bar stand right in front of Simar. She was busy licking the lemon slice with a pinch of salt. I immediately rushed to her. Now she was at the peak of being drunk. She was hardly able to open her eyes. I gave an angry look to the bartender and shouted, 'Why did you serve her?' But that was all I could do. They weren't wrong in serving her. After all, she was a patron. Also, how would they have known that it was the first time Simar was drinking alcohol! For all the problems I had faced I now wanted to make it her last day of boozing.

By now the food that I had ordered had arrived, but I had lost my appetite completely. Moreover, Simar wasn't in a condition to eat. In her semi-conscious state she had remembered to check with me about my mother and whether I managed to fool her properly!

I helped Simar in getting off the high barstool she was sitting on. 'Let's have some food. You must be hungry.'

Back in her seat she rested her head against the back of the couch. She was hardly able to keep her eyes open when she said, 'I am not hungry at all, baby.'

Later she started murmuring something. She was pleasantly talking to herself and would occasionally mutter something to me. I looked at her regretfully, thinking that had I handled the situation better and not let her get this drunk we could have had a pleasant evening. We had created enough of a scene by now and almost everyone in the restaurant had taken note of what my girlfriend was up to. I wanted to leave and therefore asked the waiter to take back the meal and pack it as a takeaway for me.

All the while Simar continued to mutter things to me, intermittently opening and shutting her eyes.

She first asked me what had happened to her and whether she was safe and all right. I held her hand in mine and said, 'You are drunk, Simar, but you are safe. You shouldn't have had those tequilas without asking me,' I expressed my displeasure mildly.

Her mind only partly registered what I was saying and she then went into another spell of sleep. The next time she woke up she complained of her head spinning. I insisted that she talk to me and not sleep. She agreed and looked into my eyes. Then she smiled and said, 'You look so cute, Ravz.' After many moments of anxiety and nervousness with her crazy antics, she brought a smile to my face.

'Can I eat your cute nose?' she flirted with me. I smiled at her and ignored her compliment.

The waiter was taking long to get my parcel and the bill. I asked someone at the bar to hurry it up. I wanted to leave as soon as possible. Right then Simar decided to announce, in her funny kiddish tone, 'Ravz, I need to go to the loo.'

'Hmmm . . . All right, there it is.' I raised my hand to show her the ladies' room and thought it would be a great way to reduce the alcohol effect in her body. But then here was the bomb.

'But I want to go with you!' she said.

'What? Ha! Ha!' I laughed at her frankness.

'You want me to help you till the door?' I offered.

'Not just the door, baby.' And she forced open her eyes to look at me.

'Then?' I said and pulled myself back.

She took a moment to compose her thoughts and then said, 'Let's go and pee together.'

I bit my tongue in my mouth. For a split second I visualized myself with her peeing in the same loo. Then I stepped back and visualized myself entering the women's room with a whole bunch of ladies staring at me. I visualized their scandalized reactions. The terror of those thoughts had actually set the pressure within me to pee.

But I could see that all Simar wanted me to do was what she expected out of me. And their seemed to be little doubt in her mind that I would do it.

'*Ravzzzzzzz! Bolo na, Ravz!*' she insisted.

'No, sweetheart, this isn't right.'

'*Kyu nahi Ravz?*' she demanded, not ready to accept my answer.

I didn't answer her and after waiting for a while she yelled like a kid '*Bolo-o-o-o-o!!*' And when I still didn't answer she continued pressurizing me, '*Bol, kyu nahi aa rahe ho tum Ravz?*'

I still didn't respond.

My facial expressions conveyed that I hadn't liked what she was doing. She calmed down for a few moments and then kicked me hard under the table with her boots.

'Ouch!' I screamed, first looking at my knee and then at Simar, wondering what she was up to.

I waited for her to apologize. Instead she smiled. It wasn't worth explaining to a drunken girlfriend about what not to do. I gave up.

'Ravz, if you aren't coming, I may do it in my jeans!'

This new threat scared the hell out of me. There was no way I could talk her out of this one.

I got up from my chair, held her hand and pulled her up. As I walked beside her, I was conscious of people staring at us. We walked from the extreme left of the dining hall to the extreme right, making our way past circular dining tables with people enjoying their food and talking about us.

As soon as Simar uttered 'Ravz' again, I forced her not to talk. 'Shhhh! Calm down! You are too loud.'

'But Ravz . . .'

'Shhhh!!!! Simar, shut up. Don't create a scene!'

As we were approaching the ladies' room, in my mind I was already preparing myself for further public embarrassment. I put my hand on Simar's shoulder to help her balance herself on her feet.

At the door of the restroom Simar went inside first. A huge sense of awkwardness froze my feet. I couldn't follow her. The best I could do was to wish that Simar would do the needful and come out quickly. But when she was inside she started shouting, '*Ravin, tum cheating kar rahe ho, na!*'

I struggled between going in to calm her down and staying outside to save myself some embarrassment. I forced myself to believe that she wasn't audible to the others.

'*Monsieur!! . . . Monsieur!!*' came a voice from behind me. I turned back to see a lady from the staff.

'Yes?' I asked and she understood that I was comfortable with English.

'Sir, our customers are having problems with your demeanour,' she said in her Chinese accent.

All right, so this was the beginning of my further embarrassment! I didn't know what to say. In India I would have simply offered 100 bucks for her to leave us alone.

'*Ravin-n-n-n-n-n!!!!!!!!!*' Simar screamed again from inside.

The lady threw her hands in the air, wondering what Simar was doing. This was enough of chaos for me. I looked back at the people in the restaurant. All eyes were on me. My reputation was no longer at stake. I think I had none by now!

'Can I help her?' she offered. I was glad to accept her offer.

As the lady went inside the restroom in anger, she slammed the door. All I kept staring at was the signboard with a girl's image on the door, below which was stencilled, in French, 'Elle' (She).

I could still hear Simar's voice. She was shouting, 'Ravz, you are such a liar . . . I wanted you to take care of me . . . and you left me in the hands of this bitch!'

I squeezed my eyes shut and prayed that time would run superfast. I wanted it all to end soon.

'You didn't even listen to what I wanted to say . . .' Simar continued to shriek from the other side of the door. I heard everything.

In no time the door opened again and the lady ran out asking me to rush in and take care of Simar.

Surprised by her body language I ran inside.

Simar had thrown up. Her head was bent low over the sink. She was still puking when I entered. Her hair, which covered her face, was soiled at the ends with the puke in the sink. There was no one apart from Simar in the restroom.

'Simar!' I shouted and ran to hold her. She was still murmuring and abusing me of cheating her. Then she suddenly felt me holding her. For a while I saw her face in the mirror. The foul smell of her puke filled the washroom. It was difficult for me to see her in that miserable condition.

In that very moment my entire fear of embarrassment ran out of me. I didn't care where I was and what people outside were thinking of me. I didn't even think of thinking anything. All I cared about was my Simar.

I rubbed her back and held her hair behind her ear. With my other hand I held one of her hands. She wasn't able to open her eyes and look at herself in the mirror. All I kept saying to her was that I was there and she was safe.

It took some time for her to catch her breath. Even when she seemed to have stopped puking I made her stand there for a while in case there was more to come.

Meanwhile, the lady very helpfully got some water. I made Simar gargle with that water and take just a sip of it. The two of us stood there for some time. She was done throwing up.

After a short while, when she felt better, she simply asked, 'Ravz, why did you leave me alone?'

I felt ashamed—even more than what I had felt while I was standing out and trying to face the people in the restaurant. Her candidness had left me with tears in my eyes. I touched her cheek and patted her. I didn't say anything. I didn't have anything to say.

The difficult time had just passed and Simar was feeling better. I had washed her hair with water and removed the minute stains from her dress with paper napkins. I felt relaxed seeing her regain her consciousness. As the two of us walked out of the restroom, nothing bothered me. I didn't hide my face from the people sitting outside. Rather, I looked them straight in the eye. I was sorry that we had spoiled their evening, but I wasn't embarrassed any more. I had already accepted that sometimes such things happen. After all, Simar hadn't done anything knowingly. She was under the influence of alcohol and my poor girlfriend was harmless to anyone. Plenty of such thoughts made me strong from inside.

We collected our takeaway and drove back. While she sat next to me, Simar apologized for her irresponsible behaviour. I rubbed her head. When she asked why she had vomited I explained that this was precisely the reason why I told her not to mix her drinks. She felt sorry from her heart. I wanted to apologize to her for cheating her at the restroom door but I didn't. I wanted to do that when she was completely back in her senses. I then made her rest her head on my shoulder as we drove back to my place.

At home, I prepared some lemonade for her. She drank that. Her eyes looked as though she badly wanted to catch up on some sleep. I asked her to change and gave her a fresh night suit from my cupboard.

I held her in my arms. As she slept comfortably, I recalled every detail of that evening—the time Simar expressed her desire to drink, the table that we chose in the restaurant, Simar's first sip of beer, the alarming phone call from her mom, the tequila shots, a drunken Simar and a panicking, embarrassed me, the mess in the restroom—every scene of that evening flashed before my eyes.

In the end I looked at my sleeping baby and felt the urge to shower all my love on her. I kissed her cheek lightly. That was the first night I felt more responsible for her. I slept cuddling her.

Seventeen

Our love story progressed with the Belgian summer. We would see each other almost every day, mostly in the evenings. If it was a weekend and Simar didn't have an exam coming up, she would come to my place in the afternoon and be there till late in the evening. Most of the time she would get her study material and spend two to three hours studying, while I completed the miscellaneous household tasks for the day.

As my stay grew longer, I even managed to buy a second-hand car. I'd been feeling the need for it since Simar had came into my life. It was a small black Renault. I was lucky that someone in our Indian community circle was going back to India and was keen on disposing of various belongings before he left, so I managed to buy this car from him at a lowered rate. Simar always referred to the Renault by its number plate—4900.

'*Ravz, 4900 ko ghumaane le chalte hain hum,*' she would say.

Occasionally, we would go to a nearby lake. We would sit on the bank and watch the ducks paddling on the water. We would see the sun set in the western horizon. She would strike various poses beside the rich green palm trees and ask me to click numerous pictures of her. When it came to pictures, she was obsessed. Her cellphone had an uncountable number of pictures, ranging from dead insects found on the road to pictures of herself trying on various dresses in the trial room of an apparel store. Some of the pictures in Simar's camera were moments captured while travelling in the car. While I would drive she would often demand my attention, asking me to pose for her camera. It was perfectly okay for her to find any location during the ride and suddenly scream at the top of her voice to make me halt the car so that she could get out to click some pictures.

One of the usual things for us to do was to drive in the late evening on the road next to my office. For some unexplained reason we loved to make out with each other inside the car. Maybe it had something to do with the romance of being together and also warmly enclosed in the interior of the car.

'I smell of you whenever I spend time with you in your car. It kinda turns me on,' Simar had once revealed.

Soon our families became aware of our romance—though strictly only the part that we made them aware of. At times, late in the evening when Simar would be with me and her mom would call up, she would lie to her and say that she was in the hostel.

'Shhhhh, Ravz! Its Mom's phone call. Don't utter a single word!' she would shout before jumping to answer the phone.

Gradually, our friends in Belgium and a few dear ones back in India got to know the truth about us. In one of the conference calls that Amardeep, Manpreet, Happy and I used to hold once a quarter, I broadcasted this breaking news to them.

There were occasions when Simar and I also fought. Most of them were sorted out in a day's time. There were some which lasted longer than that. But we would exchange some sentimental messages which would make us call off the fight and soon the quarrel would be history.

Once in a blue moon, on a weekend night, we would go out to a disco and party. But that was only when we had plenty of friends, including Sanchit with his wife and Simar's college friends, to accompany us. Late in the night, when I would go to drop Simar back to her hostel, I would park my car outside and we would go for a long walk. We simply loved doing that. The sky above us would be dark and occasionally calm. As the night proceeded, the midnight airplanes would interrupt the silence of the sky. Seeing the twinkling wings and tail lights, we both would remember India. She would turn nostalgic and ask, 'Ravzu, yaar. Why aren't they taking us along with them?' And I would rub her head lovingly.

Occasionally we would go to see an Indian movie. One of the Belgian theatres was owned by an NRI—in this case, a Gujju. Whenever a new Bollywood movie did well at the box office in India, he would put up the same as a weekend movie in his theatre. I remember when Simar and I had watched the Aamir Khan starrer *Ghajini*, she'd got completely scared while watching the scene in which the villain kills the heroine. She'd gripped my wrist and squeezed her eyes shut. I realized she was crying. I consoled her in that hall which had only Indians in the audience. It took me twenty minutes to make her believe that it was all fiction and that in reality the heroine was doing well back in India. Later at night when I'd dropped her at her hostel, she'd made me check her room thoroughly before I left. She wanted me to check if, by any chance, there was a stranger hiding in her room, just the way it had happened in the movie. Even though this seemed a bit stupid to me, I actually searched the room because she was so scared. She was relieved when I found none.

We both showed up together for all the festivals and events that the Indian community in Belgium celebrated. We spent a great deal of time together. We enjoyed each and every moment of being in love. Together we drove, we ate, we exercised, we laughed, we fought, we cried, we patched up, we confronted and we celebrated. In our best moments we made love.

Autumn was ending. The trees in the courtyard of my

office had shed the last of their leaves. It was one of those unusual Belgian afternoons when the sun and late-year rain were playing hide-and-seek. I had just got back to office after having my lunch with Simar at our regular diner. I logged into my laptop to work but I felt restless—I didn't feel like I'd be able to work for the rest of the day. There was an email for Sanchit and me sent by our account manager in India. It read:

Dear Sanchit and Ravin,

The Belgium project will now be fully operated from India. The client has agreed to double the workforce as we wanted and has extended the project for 2 more years. This is great news for us. The management here wants both of you to come back, transfer the knowledge to offshore folks and lead your respective teams from offshore.

Plan your travel back to India before the new year.

Best,
Anand

Account Manager
India Office

Eighteen

It was the evening of 25 December. The world outside my house was decorated in the shades of red, white and green— red Santa Clauses, white snow and green Christmas trees.

Simar and I too had got ourselves a small Christmas tree which we placed in the balcony of my house. She'd enthusiastically decorated it with all her heart with glittering baubles and then had even put up some cheerful coloured lights. But unlike the world outside, happiness didn't prevail within my house. All my belongings from the entire one-bedroom house had been reduced to two travel bags.

After ten months of being with each other, the time had finally come when we were to part—though only physically. Simar had been sounding low ever since I'd told her the news of my going back to India. There had been times when she wasn't able to cope with the situation and would burst into tears. I too was sad. Simar had eight more months of studies left before she could come back to India.

But I tried to cheer her up.

'Baby . . . you are anyway coming to India in your next term break, na?'

'But that's four months away, Ravz!' she wailed.

I kissed her forehead and gently rubbed her back. I looked at her closely. She seemed to be on the verge of crying, so I cracked a few jokes. The initial ones didn't work but the later ones did rescue her from her depression.

When she was able to speak a little later, she said, 'I have got something for you.'

'*Aaaiiiin?*' I pretended to be ignorant in a mischievous way.

'Hahaha . . . *Ravz, itna funny mat bano.*'

She then pulled her bag towards herself and took out a large red Santa cap. Absent-mindedly biting her lower lip—as was her typical expression—she handed over the inverted cap to me. 'This is for you,' she said.

I looked inside the cap and was amazed to see it full of big and small thermocol balls along with some cotton ribbons. I dipped my hand into the pool of fluffy thermocol to hunt for whatever was in there. I grabbed and pulled out little bells, a few trinkets, a heart, a designer pen . . .

Every time I found one little gift, Simar would clap delightedly at my success. She looked so cute doing that. It was getting difficult for me to control my emotions. On one occasion when I was about to get emotional, she shouted, 'Ravz! Cheatercock! Now you have started crying.'

And then I found a scroll inside the cap. I pulled it out and asked her what that was. To answer my question, she simply smiled and came over to sit in my lap. Slowly, she unrolled the scroll. I found five beautiful feathers within, each with their respective messages attached. The entire pamphlet looked striking. It was all Simar's creativity. The moment I looked at it, I planted a kiss on her cheek in gratitude for putting in so much of effort for me. She ignored my loving gesture and instead went ahead to explain the scroll to me in detail.

Her entire concept was amazing. Those five feathers apparently signified five great moments which I'd brought to her life in the past few months. When I wanted her to tell me about those moments she ignored me again and continued talking about the set of feathers. In her scroll she mentioned that she was so grateful for all the fantastic moments I brought to her life that she could do almost anything in return for them. And so those five feathers, she explained, marked her five promises to do anything for me in the future.

'Ravzu, you can use this first feather whenever we fight next, though I pray to god that we don't fight at all. But still, if we ever fight and then—no matter who is right and who is wrong—if you give this feather back to me, I will give up the fight and accept whatever you say.'

I was blown away by the sweetness and innocence of her thoughts. One by one, she then explained to me the purpose of all the remaining feathers. The second one was to be used when I wanted her to give up any one habit of hers. She said it was going to be tough, though, and I should try not to use that feather. I laughed in response and inhaled the scent of her hair.

'This third one, Ravzi, is when you want to make out and I am not in the mood—which rarely will be the case! But in case that is so, you can make me game with this feather!' Saying this, she held her hand over her mouth, trying to control her laughter.

I was happy for she was finally laughing.

The second last one was funny. 'This will save you one time from my mood swings during my periods.'

We both burst into a fit of laughter and I said, 'I wish I could get plenty of *this* kind of feather!'

'Shut up, Ravz!' she shouted, warning me with her eyes.

'And what's with this fifth one?' I asked, getting serious.

'This one I will let you know only once all the other four have been used.'

'Interesting,' I said and kissed her as if she was my kid. She was a darling! I was very impressed with all the hard work she'd done for me.

We didn't sleep that night but kept talking the whole night. At dawn, when it was all calm outside, Simar and I stood in my balcony. The Christmas lights still glowed in the surrounding area. The stars were about to disappear and the sky in the east was turning red when the cab arrived in the parking lot in front of my building.

It was time to say goodbye to the house in which Simar and I had created many wonderful memories which would remain with us for the rest of our lives. It wasn't easy and it was more noticeable given that the two of us were not talking much in our last few moments in that house.

In the silence of the early morning, I locked up the door of my rented apartment in Belgium for the very last time and handed the keys over to Simar who would then give them over to the landlord later in the day. Till the moment we reached the cab neither of us talked and all that was audible was the sound of our footsteps. Laughter had yet again failed to show up on Simar's face.

About an hour later, I bid Simar goodbye. I did that with the kiss she'd once taught me!

I butterfly-kissed her.

Nineteen

I was back in Chandigarh.

The change that both Simar and I felt in the initial few days was huge. All of a sudden from being in each other's company, seeing each other every day, we were now miles apart from each other. There were plenty of moments of missing each other, of mood swings and of the sudden urge to see each other. We fell upon technology to fill in the gap created by the distance that now separated us. Most of the time we would be on video chat.

The four and a half hours time difference between India and Belgium was felt more now than it used to be in the past when my parents would call me. Time-wise I was ahead of her. In the morning I would feel alone for a couple of hours. I would feel that I was wide awake in the real world while she was in her dream world of sleep, and that there was a gap between these two worlds. A seemingly unbridgeable gap.

And around 11 a.m., when I would think that Simar was getting out of her bed, I would see the gap between her world and mine being bridged. It's all psychological but then that's what it used to be with me. Not that we used to talk as soon as she used to get up, but somewhere in my subconscious mind I would feel a sense of comfort realizing that I could reach her easily now. I would feel that she was thinking about me.

I missed Simar. I missed Belgium. I missed the combination of them the most. I would recall the times I held her in my hands, or when I smelled her hair with my chin resting on her shoulder from behind. I would think of the times we roamed in the countryside of Belgium and got wet in the rain. I missed holding her in my arms; I longed to touch her soft skin.

Back in India I gradually was adapting to my old routine of living with my family. From home to office, from office to gym and from gym to home again was pretty much my usual day. My time at night was all reserved for Simar. For hours she and I would chat over the Internet via a webcam. Most of the time I would see her in her nightdress. Occasionally, when she would turn seductive, she knew what to wear and what not to wear. She would make various funny faces and I longed for the technology to transport me instantly to where she was.

'Ravz, it only happens in virtual-reality movies like *Matrix*.'

She would say that so cutely and I would instantly want to kiss her; not in virtual reality but for real.

We did make love over the phone. It used to be the only way to let ourselves loose and talk crazy. We imagined ourselves with each other and soon our imaginations would take us to a world from where we never wanted to return. I would narrate to her the scene and she would happily fill in the gaps wherever need be.

'The way you describe it, the way you choose your words, I feel it's all real,' she once said after making out over the phone.

'I know. I am an author,' I told her.

And for some unknown reason she burst into laughter. I wondered if this time I had picked the wrong words.

At times we would fight. It made the relationship feel more human. She would get irritated when I talked in Punjabi. She was never comfortable with it and I wanted her to pick it up—which, in a way, would have helped her after our marriage. She didn't like seeing me dressed in my kurta–pyjama night suit on the webcam. In Belgium she would push me to change into T-shirts and shorts but she had little say when I was in India. Simar said that this was the outcome of a long-distance relationship.

No matter what we did we missed each other. We were always on each other's mind.

This phase of longing for each other from a distance continued for a while and then the situation gradually stabilized and our daily routines started taking over our lives. I got occupied in setting up my team at the offshore office.

Simar also got busy with her exams and we chatted less frequently. After her exams, Simar came to India during her term holidays.

It is over a month since I left Belgium. It is midnight in India. Simar and I are chatting over the Internet. She says she is feeling low. I can sense that without her telling me. She is missing me. I am trying to cheer her up. She says she is not able to focus on her studies and wants me to come back to Belgium.

'Bt its been so long n I hvnt seen u . . .' she writes.

I send her my webcam request, so that she can see me and vice versa.

'Ravz, this isnt wht I want, n u knw that well. I am missing you goddamnit.'

And she ends up crying.

I don't want her to cry. It hurts me to see tears in her eyes. I can't bear to see any pain on her cute face. I want to take her in my arms and kiss her forehead as if she is my baby.

'Simar . . . no sweetie. It's jst a matter of 4 more mnths. N after that we wll always b together.'

It takes me a little while to calm her down. She has stopped crying but is not saying anything. She doen't want to chat any more and wants to be alone.

'Btw wen u'll b here, shall I come to ur place in gurgaon or will u b comin to chandigarh?' I ask this only to distract her from her misery by involving her in conversation.

'Ravz pls u come na. Coz in d night u can stay with ur frnd MP in gurgaon. If I come I won't find ny place 2 halt in the night.'

After crying, her face looks dry with her tear-stained cheeks and heavy eyes. But she does fine as I hold her attention and continue to talk with her.

'Yes b4 marriage our families won't allow us to spend a nite at each oder's place. But if u come to Chd I'll arrange a hotel for you.'

'Ravz . . . wch hotel?'

I don't answer her but watch her on my screen.

'Bolo na, Ravz . . . hotel taj?'

'No baby.'

'Hmmm . . . thn hotel marriott?'

'No dear.'

'Then which hotel Ravziiiiiii?' she writes back and raises her hands in the air.

'Hotel Decent ;-),' I say.

And she bursts into laughter, recalling the plot of the movie that we once watched together.

When she is able to catch her breath again, she playfully quotes a dialogue from the film, 'Ravz, hum room ghantey ke hisaab se lengey ki purey din ke liye?'

She laughs again, this time at her own statement, and doesn't even bother to listen to my answer. I feel satisfied to see her laughing again.

Twenty

Simar was back in Gurgaon and she had planned to make me meet her parents.

I boarded the Chandigarh–Delhi Shatabdi and then took a metro from Delhi to Gurgaon. The metro ride was good. It was my first ride in the metro which had recently started plying in the city. The whole idea of rushing across a city in a capsule that travels both under the earth as well as high above the ground, and which yet remains so neat and clean—something we seldom associate with trains in India—was exciting. It was fast and hence rather different from the local Indian trains. The only similarity was the uncountable Indian population which somehow manages to squeeze its way into the coach. I was fascinated by the kinds of announcements being made within the metro—first in Hindi, followed by its translation in English. But more than all this, that entire morning I felt this excitement of seeing her again after so long a time. It was a different feeling altogether.

Near about noon I reached her place. I had been talking to her over the phone to find the directions to her house. As I reached my final destination for the day, I saw her from a distance standing at the main gate of her house.

I smiled. Seeing me, she waved.

It was a tender moment which had come after so long a time. I was finally seeing my Simar. She too was impatiently waiting for me. I ran towards her with the flowers in my hand that I'd brought for her. Simar was visibly delighted to see me right in front of her eyes. After a run of about fifty-odd yards, I was breathing fast. It was a moment of celebration for both of us—and a very emotional one too. I satisfied the thirst in my eyes and looked at her from head to toe. It was incredible to see her, to touch her and to hear her next to me once again. She was as beautiful as I had left her in Belgium. She first looked here and there to check if anyone was staring in the neighbourhood, then gave me a quick hug. I enjoyed that brief unexpected surprise and lost myself in the warmth of her touch which I had missed so much in the past few months. I wanted it to last longer. It was different yet special to be together again—different because the environment around us was so unlike that of Belgium; and special because we got together again after a long interval.

It took me a while to shift my attention from Simar to her house. It was a huge bungalow with a sprawling and lush green lawn. There was a wooden swing in one corner of the lawn with a few cane chairs surrounding it. A Honda CRV and an Audi were parked in the garage on the left.

She took me inside her house and it was something to be admired. It was luxurious, spacious and well designed with nice interiors. At a distance I saw her parents approaching us.

'You never told me you are that rich!' I whispered and elbowed her.

'Shut up!' she said and pinched my back.

In a few seconds, her parents were right in front of me. I touched their feet. Simar made the necessary introductions.

Her dad, I came to know, was a businessman and was running some telecom business. I was already aware of this but Simar seemed to want to update me one more time. I don't know why she would sometimes get extra formal like this. Her dad was tall and well built. But he looked slightly older than what he looked like in the family pictures that Simar had shown me. Her mom on the other hand looked exactly like how she appeared in those same pictures. She was fair and slim. Simar clearly got her looks from her mom. Her mom was a lawyer. I was already aware of this as well but then there was no point in stopping Simar. I allowed her to repeat, all over again, everything she had once told me about her family. It was like copy-pasting from the past.

'Where is your dog, Simar?' I asked when she forgot to copy-paste this part of her family story. And I found there was no pasting required this time.

'He died, Ravz, about two months ago,' she said sadly. 'I only got to know yesterday.'

I hung my head low, thinking I would score some brownie points from her dad if he noticed me sharing their grief.

'I miss him and now I want to get a new one. But Dad hates pets!' Simar said and, in less than thirty seconds, thus ruined the position of advantage I thought I had.

Simar's dad was to leave for a workshop in a few hours and her mom had taken leave from her office so that she could meet me.

We talked a lot over lunch. We talked about how Simar and I met. We talked about my career and goals. We talked about my novel.

'I heard from Simar that your novel is a bestseller,' her dad asked.

'Ah . . . Yes,' I softly answered without boasting about it.

'It's titled *I Too Had a Love Story*, right?' her mom asked this time.

'Hanji.'

'Hmm . . . I will read it soon though Simar narrated the storyline to me last night. It takes guts to pen down an emotional tale, young man,' her dad pitched in.

I didn't say anything for I didn't know what to say.

Later in the evening, when Simar and her mom were back in their rooms, her dad and I walked out in the lawn. It was pleasantly cloudy outside. In one corner the gardener was digging the earth to plant a few saplings. There were quite a few domestic servants in that house—a watchman, a gardener and a maid.

'I found you to be a nice guy, Ravin,' her father said.

I looked up to his face as he continued, 'And Simar is our only child. She has been brought up with a lot of affection.'

'I know,' I responded.

From there it was almost as if a round of one-to-one conversation had begun between her dad and me. The last thing he said, before we sat for the late-afternoon tea, was, 'At times Simar doesn't know what she actually wants. It's very important for you to ask her on how both of you plan to live your lives together. In my short interaction with her today I found that she is yet to talk to you about a lot of things. I hope both of you have a common path.'

Her dad left me thinking about what his words exactly meant. It wasn't quite clear what he was trying to convey to me. I struggled with my curiosity and desire to understand what he had meant by this chat. But then my doubts simply disappeared the moment I saw Simar laughing openly and coming towards us. She was with her mother and was carrying a bowl of dry fruits. The maid was following the ladies with a tea tray and some light snacks.

Her dad quickly finished the tea and left for his workshop.

Simar, her mom and I chatted for a while. It was late in the evening when I left her place. Apart from the last few words that her dad had said to me, everything else had been great. Overall, I was happy to have met her family.

I didn't go home after that. As per my plan, I headed straight to meet Manpreet. He was working with an IT firm in Gurgaon itself and this was the best time to catch up with him. It was more than a year since we had last met.

It was great to see him again and remember our college days. Manpreet raised a toast to my courtship with Simar. We boozed till late in the night. Meanwhile, we set up a conference call in which we got Amardeep from Hyderabad and Happy from London. It turned out to be a crazy night full of banter, laughter and male bitching.

Twenty-one

While on holiday, Simar came once to Chandigarh for a day's visit. For some reason, she wasn't in a mood to come but I had strongly persuaded her to come and visit my mother. It was just my mom and me in Chandigarh. My dad was out of station that day and my brother was in the US working at his client's location for the past ten months.

On my insistence, Simar was also wearing a traditional salwar–kameez. I knew she wore that only on a few occasions. I always found her to look very pretty in Indian attire. On the day she arrived, I picked her up from the railway station and we drove to my place.

Those days we used to live in a rented apartment in Chandigarh. As the two of us walked in, Simar looked at the entire house and reserved her comments. It was certainly a small house; very small compared to her own.

'Three more months and my brand new flat will be ready.

If time permits I will show it to you today,' I said, sensing her discomfort and hence trying to help save the situation.

'Oh yes, Ravz, I forgot to ask about your upcoming flat. Great to know that!' she exclaimed joyfully.

Meanwhile, my mother entered the living room. She had been at our landlady's place for their regular chit-chat.

I introduced Simar to my mom. They began with the common pleasantries. I preferred to stay quiet and to pitch in only when needed. My mom was quite happy to meet Simar. A little later she served us some juice and some eatables and we settled down again in the living room.

Unlike the atmosphere at her place, the mood at my place was quite cool and relaxed. Or maybe it was just me who felt that way—after all, I was in my own home. I narrated a few humorous incidents from the time Simar and I lived in Belgium and we all laughed. Primarily, I wanted to make Simar comfortable, which I succeeded in doing. So much so that she started complaining to my mom about the little things I did in Belgium that had bothered her. My mom kept laughing. And at times when she wasn't laughing or listening to Simar's short stories from Belgium, she kept asking Simar about her family and kept telling her about my dad and my brother.

We interacted for a long time before mom asked me to get some dessert from the market to have after lunch. I left Simar and my mom to talk in privacy.

The next time the three of us were together was later in

the afternoon when we were preparing to sit at the dining table for lunch. Simar had wanted to help my mom with the cooking, but she didn't have any idea how to help her. Back in Belgium, when it came to who would do the cooking, I was the obvious choice. So now, to rescue Simar from embarrassment, I strategically asked her to do the salad dressing as part of the entire cooking episode.

'Thank you!' she whispered in my ear.

'Muah!' I kissed her cheek without my mom noticing.

She panicked when she realized that I just kissed her with my mom a foot away from us in the kitchen. She glared at me and tried to shove me away. I did the opposite. I went closer and pinched her on the butt. She looked shocked while I continued to smile mischievously, and all the while my mom remained unaware of this, being distracted by the whistle of the pressure cooker.

'Aunty, where are the tomatoes and cucumber?' Simar asked cleverly to attract my mother's attention and hence put an end to whatever naughtiness I was involved in.

Soon we were eating. My mom had cooked a delicious lunch.

'*Aunty, lunch to bahut hi tasty banaaya hai aapne!*' Simar said.

And that was a trigger to my mom to offer her more paneer and raita. Simar refused but her resistance failed as my mother insisted on serving her some more. I smiled at Simar's helplessness when she looked at me.

'*Aajkal ke bachchey kuch khaate hi nahi hai,*' is all my mom said.

Simar was quick to learn that there was no need to say no now.

It was about 2.30 p.m. and we were through with our lunch. Luckily, the weather was pleasant outside. Simar was to catch the evening Shatabdi back to Delhi.

'Let me show you Chandigarh,' I said, getting up.

'At this time? Take some rest, na?' my mom suggested.

'Ma, her train is at 6.15 in the evening. We don't have much time on our hands,' I explained.

But my mom still forced us to sit for a while with her. I agreed, saying, 'In that case we won't be coming back home and I will drop her at the station in the evening before I come back.'

My mom was okay with it. I did ask her to join us, but I think she thought it wiser to give us both some much-needed private time.

In less than half an hour we were in the renowned Sector 17 market of Chandigarh.

'Ravz! This is such a European-style market, yaar. It's beautiful!' she gushed.

'You like it?' I asked

'Oh! I love it!' she answered.

We bought two ice-cream cones and took a full round of the market. We didn't buy anything but enjoyed window shopping.

I tried to show her as much of Chandigarh as possible. Later in the day we crossed the famous rock garden but didn't actually visit it, given the paucity of time. Instead we went to Lake Sukhna.

We parked the vehicle and entered the lake area through the main entrance. There were small restaurants operating at the entrance and some small stalls with vendors selling a variety of eatables and toys for the kids. Given the time at which we had arrived, there weren't many people there. Usually it is late in the evening when the lake attracts a large crowd.

We walked past the entrance and headed towards the shore of the lake. It was calm. On one side nature offered rich greenery with beautiful palm trees, bonsais and multicoloured flowers, and on other side it offered us a soothing expanse of water. The placid lake, with the hills of Kasauli behind it, wonderfully filled our sight. The silent water in the lake reflected the clouds in the sky above. The audio speakers installed every twenty metres on the path along the shore treated our ears with the gentle melody of classical music. Occasionally, the quacks of a herd of ducks paddling in the lake would drown out the sound of the classical music.

'Wow!' she exclaimed when she looked at the lake and the surrounding greenery. 'This is such a breathtaking experience.'

The lake brought back memories of our time together in Belgium. We recalled how, at times, we used to go to the lake in Mechelen. We walked by the side of the lake, hand in hand.

'After marriage we will come here frequently,' I said.

She didn't acknowledge my statement. Strangely, I found the smile on her face fading when she heard this. I looked at her, wondering what had happened.

'Ravz, I wanted to ask you something,' she said.

'Ask me then,' I said, wondering what had come to her mind all of a sudden.

'Are we going to live in Chandigarh after marriage?'

I stopped walking when I heard that and faced her.

'What do you mean by that, Simar?' I responded with a question. 'Of course we are!'

'Ravz, I thought we will settle down in Belgium.'

'What?' I burst into laughter. 'What has happened to you, Simar?'

'I am studying there. I will get a fabulous job there.'

'We will get married only once you complete your studies and you can get a fabulous job here in India as well.'

She didn't say anything for a while but kept silent, as though deep in thought. We again started walking.

'Ravz, I don't want to get married immediately after my studies. I want to work for a year,' she pleaded suddenly.

'Simar! What has happened to you, baby? During our discussions in Belgium, I always expressed my desire to settle down once you come back to India. And you seemed to agree.'

'But I think it is important for a girl to get some job experience before her marriage life starts. It will be difficult later.'

'But you have already worked for two years before you got admitted into the business school. It is not going to be difficult. And even if it appears difficult, I am okay with you getting into a job first; but I don't want to wait for one full year after you graduate.'

I found Simar a little insecure about her future. I had never seen her that way. I thought about comforting her as well but I wasn't sure what actually was bothering her. We talked some more.

'But sweetheart,' I continued, 'you can do all that here in India as well, na? Don't your parents want you to be close to them?'

'My dad is planning to wrap up his business from India and join my chaachu in Belgium. But it will take some time.'

'Oh, I see . . . You mean your entire family will move to Belgium?'

'Yes. Sooner or later.'

I now understood where she was coming from. A little later I politely mentioned, 'But Simar, I can't move to Belgium. I had only gone there to work on one of the company's on-site projects. I will have plenty of other such trips to Belgium and other countries in the future. But when it comes to settling down, I want to settle down here in Chandigarh. I had told you about the flat I have been constructing for us.'

Neither of us said anything for some time.

Breaking the recently introduced silence, I asked, 'Since when have you been wishing to settle down abroad?'

'Ever since I was there, Ravz.'

'But you never mentioned this to me, Simar.'

She looked away to the waters of the lake. She took a few seconds to respond. 'Because I thought it was implicit. We met in Belgium and we lived together in Belgium. I thought we will continue to live there forever.'

'But whenever I used to talk about what I wished for our future I would always tell you how we would live with my family in India. You never said anything then. Are you now saying that you can't live without your parents and that's why you want to settle down there?'

'Sort of,' she quickly answered.

'But you have been living there for close to two years pursuing your MBA without your parents and without any hassles.'

She didn't have much to say and opted to keep silent. I wanted to understand her inhibitions in detail but somehow her reasons didn't appear perfect. With our discussion having lasted longer than we had planned, we had to cancel the plan to show her my upcoming flat. My wristwatch told me that we were getting late. I wrapped up the subject without being able to get to the root of the issue and without being able to convince her. But I did give her substantial reasoning to change her mind. 'I have to take care of my parents. They are getting old and my dad will soon be retiring. My brother is going to apply for a US green card and he will be settling there. My parents won't be comfortable spending their old age abroad. That lifestyle would be very unsuitable for them.'

Back in the car I changed the subject and was able to cheer her mood, saying, 'Don't worry, baby, things will work out because at the end of the day we love each other.'

At the Chandigarh railway station, she boarded the Shatabdi. I stood on the platform till the train left the station. It is quite a different feeling to see off your beloved and go back home alone. I recalled the time she'd done the same for me when I was leaving for the airport in Belgium.

Twenty-two

'Bt wat's wrong with being in India?'

'It's diff for me to adjust there Ravz.'

Simar was back in Belgium and we were back to chatting over the Internet.

The days which Simar spent in India passed by in the blink of an eye. It was certainly a very short time that she and I had together in India but, nevertheless, it proved to be a very valuable period during which we got to meet each other's families. However, the discussion that we had on the shore of the lake in Chandigarh was still not over. It had lasted longer than I had expected. But I was more worried because of the course it was gradually taking.

'Adjust????'

'I . . . I don't knw Ravz bt I feel more comfortable here.'

'N wat r ur reasons behind this comfort there?'

'Coz I've bn here for the past 2 years.'

'U were in India for 22 years, so don't gv me tht reason Simar . . .'

She didn't respond to my statement. When Simar had first mentioned settling down abroad I thought she was kidding. And if not that, I thought it was perhaps one of her kiddish whims and that I would soon convince her to change her mind. But even twenty days later, Simar stuck firmly to her viewpoint, pushing me to buy her argument—an argument which lacked fundamental reasoning.

'Plz Ravz . . . I hv dreamt of being here. I hv dreamt of livin my life with u here. D time tht we hv spent here with u makes me live here with u. I wanna work here n visit entire Europe with u. I hv this dream . . .'

And I cut her mid-sentence: 'N wat bout my dreams Simar? Wat bout my new flat in Chandigarh?'

'Ur parents will live there na.'

'Bt I don't wanna make them live alone. They r getting old and they wl need us to tk care of them.'

As usual I wasn't able to change her mind. I wasn't against her dreams but I wanted her to have realistic dreams which were not built at the cost of ruining the essential needs in our lives. All of a sudden leaving a country with no proper reasoning didn't seem like the right thing to do. And I wasn't able to understand why she never expressed her willingness to settle in Europe before. But what I had understood by now was that this wasn't yet another of her mood swings. She was totally serious about it.

Our discussion on this subject didn't continue for just a few days; we argued for more than a month. And nothing seemed to have changed at the end of it. I had never thought that Simar and I could ever debate on a single subject for so long. It was certainly the first time this had happened. Everything has a first time. That's what life is all about, I thought.

'Where women are concerned, the unexpected is always expected.'

It was Happy who said this to me while I was discussing my present condition with him. In the end he and I just laughed. He didn't have anything else to offer me.

Things did not get any smoother from then onwards. In fact, with every passing day the matter got even more serious. It was unbelievable how little things were turning everything sour. I wanted to stop it. I was badly looking for reasons to buy her argument which time and again I failed to get. In that period Simar and I had experienced a range of emotions, from shouting at each other to not talking the day after, from crying uncontrollably to finally comforting each other. The winds of our relationship had taken a different course. The season of romance had begun to witness something that it had never witnessed before.

~

When Simar first came into my life, I was almost lifeless. Deep in my heart I was still mourning the loss of my first love. Simar brought me back to life. She had not just brought back happiness in my life—she was the sole happiness in my life.

With this thought in my mind I gradually started to put myself in her shoes and tried to see the kind of life she wanted to live with me. To be honest, I started discounting the illogical part of her argument and started considering the merits that her demand had for both of us.

If Simar is not happy, I wouldn't be happy either—I started thinking that way.

My theory that wealth, women and wine—or at least one of them—will surely be a man's weakness, again held true.

And, unfortunately, I was the man here, and she was a woman; she was my weakness. And there was a reason to turn weak.

I had already lost my love once. I didn't want to lose it again.

One evening, when I was a little high on alcohol, I wrote Simar an email.

To the girl who taught me how to butterfly kiss!

The past few months have been terrible for both of us. And, baby, I have missed you a lot! I don't know how difficult it would be for me to settle down in Europe. But I think it will be less difficult than seeing you unhappy.

I want to lead a wonderful life with you. But I cannot

deny the fact that I have responsibilities on my shoulders. And I want to balance my responsibilities and my life. I want to see you happy. Give me some time and let me see what opportunities I have to move to Belgium.

Yours,
Ravz

Twenty-three

Having done my share of sacrifice, life appeared to have moved back on track. For Simar, it was as if all her wishes had come true. She would thank me numerous times and whenever she would describe our future life she would add something new to her stack of dreams. She would tell me how we would decorate our living room, what all we would cook when it rained, where all we would go to spend our holidays and a lot more. At times she would race so ambitiously in her dreams that she would talk about big houses, expensive cars and luxurious lifestyles. Sometimes her imagination would scare me with the high level of expectations. But then, in the end, I would ignore those fears, telling myself that she was yet again simply fantasizing about the future and it was only natural that she would want me to be a part of her dreams. There was nothing to fear in that, I would tell myself. After all, just because she was voicing these concerns now did not mean that all these changes must happen overnight! At best, I would think, at least she was optimistic and wished for a good future.

While she kept dreaming and concentrating on her MBA at the same time, I flung into action on things I needed to do before I could pack my bags in India. There were plenty of things on my to-do list which needed attention, of which my job, my family and my flat were the top priority.

My whole idea was to align all these upcoming changes with the biggest upcoming change in my life—the marriage. Considering the adjustments I had made in my life to accommodate Simar's expectations, it seemed more practical for Simar and me to finalize our marriage. But whenever I raised this subject, Simar tended to put this matter on the back burner especially since her final term exams were right on top of her list of priorities. She said she wanted peace of mind to think over it.

I thought it would be wise to let Simar concentrate on her exams and, rather, to take her parents' opinion on this subject. Thinking this, I called up her dad in Gurgaon. As I dialled his number I recalled our last meeting at his house and the words he'd spoken to me back then.

After the initial pleasantries I updated him on what all had happened between Simar and me in the last few days and how I was planning to shift to Belgium. Apparently he was already aware of the situation through Simar.

He listened to me patiently as I told him of the main purpose of my call—I was talking about marriage.

'Hmm . . . What about your flat which was under construction?' he asked.

'I will soon be getting possession of it and, most probably before we leave India, I will be renting it out.'

'And what about your parents, Ravin?'

'They will join me. I am yet to talk to them, but I believe I will be able to convince them.'

'Hmm . . . I would be very happy if that happens, Ravin. But is Simar aware of this?'

'Aware of what, Uncle?'

'That your family will be joining you?'

'I am not sure if we have explicitly talked about this, but, more or less, she should be aware of this. But why are you asking this question?'

Her dad took a deep breath before he spoke again,

'Ravin, I know that Simar insisted you move to Belgium, but when she asked you to do this, did you try to find out why she wanted to do so?'

'I asked her and whatever reasons she gave me appeared unreasonable to me. Maybe the way she dreams of her future life . . .' I left my answer incomplete.

Simar's dad waited for a while, allowing me to speak further. But I didn't. And very calmly, he spoke again.

'Ravin, if you remember when you were here I did mention to you that, for a successful life together, it is of the utmost importance for life partners to be on the same page.' He continued further, saying, 'I had told you that Simar is a pampered kid. At times she is very demanding and I am sure by now you would have realized it. The other thing is that Simar has always wanted her own space which she relates to her independence. This is something she is very particular about. The hard fact is that she wanted to settle down abroad because she wanted to live with just you.'

'What do you mean just me?' I asked.

'Talk to her about this. You really should.'

As her dad spoke further, I was beginning to understand Simar's actual reasons to move out of India. She didn't want to live with my family but wanted just the two of us to live together. A series of Simar's dreams flashed in my mind and I recalled that none had a vision of living with my parents. She had never mentioned anything about us living with them. On the contrary, I recalled always saying to her that we will take care of our parents and be under their blessings. She knew how much I valued family and relations. She also knew that my parents wouldn't be willing to move out of India.

As the blurred image of Simar's wishes was getting clear in front of my eyes I was starting to feel uncomfortable. I didn't have much to say. I simply kept listening to her dad who was merging the broken links to explain to me what I hadn't fully understood till now.

'Simar has done well in life. We have always shown her the path on which she should walk ahead in life. Most of the time she has accepted the path, but then she has preferred to walk alone. She has always preferred staying in hostels, even when she was here in Delhi. And we accepted her wishes, knowing that she is not ruining her life in any way. She is an independent person and wants to live her life in her own way. And I don't see a problem in it as long as she is able to live in prosperity. My only problem is that she keeps such thoughts close to her heart and I suppose she wouldn't have shared this with you. While I move my entire business to Belgium, Simar wants you to join my business. As a matter of fact, she wants both you and herself to take this business ahead. She wants you to leave your job.'

I was in the dark when it came to many of the stories which Simar's dad was sharing with me that day over the call. If all he had been saying was correct, then it was shocking for me to find out the truth this way. I felt this sudden urge to call Simar and make her clarify everything to me.

The tone in which her dad had spoken was compelling. It was very considerate and good of him to share those facts with me. Somewhere I realized that even Simar's family had adjusted to a life as per Simar's wishes. Before I hung up, having listened to a few more facts about Simar, I asked her dad why they didn't simply push and convince her the way she would convince them. His reply was crisp.

'I wish we had done that earlier on in her life. It's too late now. Not that she wouldn't agree to do what we say, but that she would end up crying each and every day. I know her. And as a father it is difficult to see your child that way. It has happened umpteen times in the past.'

The entire conversation I had that evening with Simar's

father left me wondering. In the first go, I wanted to call Simar, but then later I decided against doing so. I thought it was better to prepare myself before I got to hear from Simar whether all that I had heard was right. How could she? And why would she? I kept thinking to myself the whole night. Sleep was miles away from me—and so was Simar. I wanted to stop her, explain to her before she went too far away—so far that it would be impossible to get her back. I kept turning in my bed the whole night.

In the morning I went to make some tea for myself. I had a severe headache. I was still going over the entire conversation from the evening before. I kept watching the flame on the stove.

The words 'She doesn't want to live with your family, but just you' echoed in my head.

'She wants you to come and join my business and live with us,' her dad had said.

As I stood absent-mindedly in my kitchen, staring into the blue flame, the tea boiled over in the vessel. I wanted to stop it from spilling over the rim but wasn't able to do so. I wanted to stop a lot of things from spilling over. I was finding it difficult to do so.

A sudden urge, a sudden frustration and a sudden suffocation—all seemed to be running through me all at once. I called up Simar.

It was very early in the morning in Belgium. I knew I was going to wake her up from her sleep. But it didn't bother me.

Twenty-four

It took her a while to shake off her deep sleep before she could make any sense of what I was saying. I told her to freshen up and call me back, and this is exactly what she did.

Soon we were discussing the entire matter. In the initial minutes Simar didn't give me a straight answer but when I probed her more by putting my questions in different words, I realized Simar's father had been right in whatever he had said.

'And I thought it was all over when I assured you of my plans of coming to Belgium.'

We went into a debate.

She became defensive and fired a range of questions at me for the very first time: 'Will I be allowed to work and lead my life the way I am doing now? There can be chances that your mother would want me to be a homemaker!'; 'Your family is quite religious and conservative. Will I get to wear anything and everything?'; 'You had mentioned that we will have to look after your parents. There will be plenty of responsibilities and expectations. And I wish to spend the entire time with you!'; 'There will be so many restrictions in a joint family. Will we still be able to go to late night parties?'

And in the end she even had ready her own answer to all her questions: 'I won't be comfortable in a joint family, Ravin.'

I wondered how merely living with my parents meant being part of a joint family. More importantly, I was taken aback by the range of insecurities that Simar had been carrying in herself all along. I was greatly disappointed with her understanding of the subject as well as her judgement on it, especially when she had arrived at these conclusions without even discussing them with me.

When it was my turn to speak I was very careful, deciding not to be angry but to remain cool. I wanted to work on pacifying her insecurities as they weren't right. My family and I were sure that Simar would be working after marriage. I wanted her to wear everything that she was wearing when she was with her own parents. I certainly wanted to take care of my parents because they were growing old. It is a responsibility which I believe every child should adhere to. But that in no way was going to make our life miserable. I understood the meaning of privacy and freedom but I only valued them when they were taken in a justified way—that is, not at the cost of one's commitments.

With every reason I gave Simar, I was sure that I meant whatever I said. But for some reason she wasn't convinced. Her sixth sense was biased towards her own viewpoint, primarily because that is what she wanted and she valued her intuition more than my reasonable logic. The more reasonable I tried to be, the more unreasonable her questions became:

'What if I will be asked to cook for everyone?'

And to this, I answered, 'Simar, if both of us will be working, then both of us will be tired by the end of the day; and if being a guy I don't have the strength to work in the kitchen, how would I expect the same from a girl?'

'But you do cook, Ravin. You were cooking for yourself after work in Belgium.'

'Yes, because that was the need of the moment. I was all alone. Here in India we can afford maids to do the household chores. Why are you bothered that much?'

The more I was trying to finalize our marriage, the more I was discovering layers of Simar's latent expectations and fears. I felt as if a lot between us was changing. The days of our romance and laughter appeared to be very far back in the past. Our love story had entered a new phase of expectations, demands and debates.

'No! Never! Don't even of think of me leaving my parents.'

'It's not that I want you to leave your parents. I simply want an arrangement where the two of us live together and we visit them at regular intervals.'

She made no sense. I started getting furious over all her nonsense.

'And look at you, Simar! You wanted me to come and live with your family. How sick is that? You wanted me to join your dad in his business.'

'That's because you and I will have a great life. We will have our own business; we can live in a big house. Think of the luxury of life and the ease.'

'What has happened to you, Simar? When I was in Belgium did you even bother about the small rented apartment I used to be in? Did you even care for a big house, a big car and a big lifestyle then?'

'Ravz, I love you. But I also want to live a good life and have a grand lifestyle. And if both of us can get that, what's the harm in it?'

I paused for a while. I thought about what had happened so far and what was happening right at that moment. Since when did everything start changing, I wondered. Since the time I left Belgium and Simar had to live alone, I thought to myself. Maybe because that was the first time Simar was far away from me and this distance was making her reassess her priorities and think about what she actually wanted in life. Or maybe she started feeling differently once she was back in India when she had talked to her parents about all this or maybe when she visited my place.

Something in me choked. Whatever we talked about was very unpleasant for me to hear, more so because it was Simar at the other end of the conversation. I was clueless. It was hard to believe if she was the same Simar whom I loved and cared for. She had changed.

I was clear about what all she said and what all she didn't say. For everything that was happening I finally had started answering my own questions.

Simar came from a wealthy family. For a while she happened to fall in love with a guy who wasn't as wealthy as her family was but was doing reasonably well in his life. Not that she wanted to live without me, but she wanted to be with me as well as cherish all her dreams. She had always visualized a great life with all sorts of luxuries. She didn't want to compromise on that. Back in Gurgaon her family was well known and her parents had a great social network with politicians and businessmen. On the contrary, my parents hardly had any such reputation. If asked something in English, my parents most probably wouldn't even understand the question, forget about being able to answer it fluently. That, surely, was in huge contrast to her family's status and lifestyle. How then could Simar adjust with my family? My dad didn't wear a tuxedo. He'd always worn a humble kurta–pyjama all his life. My family had a simple lifestyle, not that any of us had any issues with the modern Westernized lifestyle. While in our family my mom would cook, in Simar's family they had the maids to cook and do all the work. Things were certainly different. But not so different that they would become a bottleneck, given the fact that I had always been clear with Simar about my life and my expectations. In spite of subtle differences nothing was going to prohibit Simar from living a life that she used to live so far. I lived in the same family and I had enjoyed all the freedom I wanted. And belonging to the same family I had imbibed the values and upbringing that made Simar fall in love with me. How could the same lifestyle go against her?

Things kept deteriorating between us. I didn't know where I was wrong and where Simar was right. But I still knew that we needed to work it all out. Simar's exams were round the corner and hence we called a ceasefire on this subject. We took a break, so that she could concentrate on her studies and rethink everything once she was free.

The only ray of hope had been when she spoke those final words: 'Ravz, give me some time. Let me complete my exams, and with you I want to work on my fears and insecurities.'

~

Uncertainties hovered over our fate. Time and again Simar mentioned that she knew I was right and that she would try her best to accept things, but reality was different from promises made in the throes of love. I knew things were going the other way and they were going fast. And I wanted to stop this change. I planned to take a break from my work and go to Belgium as soon as her exams finished. Simar still had a consulting project to work on after her final exams because of which she wouldn't be able to immediately travel back to India after her final exams. I wanted to discuss things face-to-face with Simar and therefore I considered this a much-needed trip.

But when things are against you, no matter what you do, they are actually against you. For some reason—call it Murphy's law, I guess!—I got to know that Simar's consulting project demanded her to visit Canada.

'Believe me, Ravin, I had no idea that they will ask me to travel all the way to Canada. At the last moment the client changed their outsourcing plan.'

It was a test of my patience. For various reasons it was no longer feasible to be together and discuss things face-to-face. I found that I started focusing less on my work and more on how to bridge the growing gap in our relationship while Simar was far more focused on her career than on working out our problems. I was still okay with that. I didn't want her to play with her career.

From her final exams that wait had now stretched to the end of her consulting project.

'Two more months, Ravz!' she had told me.

But our emotions didn't wait for that long a time. We ran through a spate of terrible moments. The vacuum I felt within was enormous. We fought and we missed each other, we cried and we held each other responsible. It was an undefined state we were in. At times we made wild love over the phone. When there is a vacuum, it feels as though a wild gush of wind—brutal and cold—runs in to fill up the space. But in the end we found ourselves at the same hurdle. We both were on the opposite side of a wide gap.

Love, like life, is so insecure. It moves in our lives and occupies its sweet space in our hearts so easily. But it never guarantees that it will stay there forever. Probably that's why it is so precious.

Twenty-five

The consulting project unfortunately stretched on for an additional three months, making it a total of five months. That was a long time. In our case, long enough to bring our relationship to the verge of falling apart. That's the brutal truth.

It was difficult for me to wait for her. It was difficult for me to forget her. I think the most difficult thing was to decide whether to wait for her or to forget her.

But the unexpected was no more unexpected. It was all clear.

My wait to finalize the marriage turned infinite. The prime reason behind this was that Simar's list of concerns had turned infinite. The more I had stretched myself the more I was further expected to stretch. Unable to accept my wish of wanting to live with my family, and thus finding it difficult to marry me, Simar gave birth to newer issues. Some were stupid enough.

'How do I live with a non-vegetarian? You are an atheist whereas I wanted my life partner to believe in God. Also I need more time as I am thinking of doing my PhD now.'

I was an atheist and I was a non-vegetarian when she was first attracted towards me. Overnight these attributes had started bothering her. I well remembered one of her last calls. She didn't even think twice before saying that one of her concerns was that she would be known as the second girl in my life, when the rest of the world knew about Khushi and me.

'On various social networking websites every fan of yours talks and will continue to talk about Khushi and you for ages.'

She wanted me to make her feel comfortable about all that. In a way she meant that my same book—which she had once loved and which had made her fall for me—was now bothering her, because it had my memories of my dead girlfriend.

I didn't say anything. My silence spoke a thousand words. She didn't hear any of them.

I hung up the call. There was no need to explain anything. She had pierced my heart with whatever she had said.

~

One can go miles to get the love of his life and then sacrifice a great deal to keep that love alive. And I too had done that when I was ready to settle down abroad, when I promised Simar her entire independence, when I said that: 'For you I can even turn vegetarian and you are so precious for me, that I will push myself to regain my faith in God only if you are there with me.'

When you are in love, you tend to think from the heart. That's what I kept doing for most of the time. The sad part was that it was just me who kept doing that. But a relationship only works when both the people are willing to make sacrifices. I wanted to be her better half and not her slave. Unlike her, I didn't have a long list of clauses which she had to fulfil before she could marry me. I simply wished for the obvious to happen and for her to accept my family. But that one wish was unacceptable to her, and became a bottleneck in our relationship. It turned everything between us sour.

Someone said it right: change is the only constant. With time, things change, seasons change and, amidst a list of change-prone entities, we surely read that people change too.

By the time Simar actually came back to India after her consulting assignment, things had boiled down to a yes or no decision. It was paradoxical how we ended up having nothing left to say to each other when, some time back, we couldn't stop ourselves from talking to each other. The present condition threw a lot of questions on the truth of the love we were in. Was it all real?

The problem with being in love is that you find it difficult to survive without the other person. No matter how many times you decide not to succumb to it, you eventually land up trying one more time. Things would have been simpler for humans if we were born with only a brain. The addition of heart has brought in all the complexities in my case.

I kept my fingers crossed and I kept them crossed for long.

It is night. From behind the wheel, I keep looking at the date on the dashboard of my car. I am shocked to look at it and realize how cursed it is for me. I am not able to move my eyes away from it. I rest there in my car for a long time. I am feeling suffocated and breathing heavy. I have rolled down the windowpanes. I feel as if something sharp has just been stabbed in my chest. And I am hanging in that tense but short period between being hit and feeling the terrible ache that follows. I know it is going to hurt in a very short while. As if some kind of poison is going to run in my veins and paralyse me. I am split seconds away from that terrible pain. Probably that's why I am scared to look anywhere else and, instead, am left staring at that date. A lump of saliva in the back of my mouth gets stuck in my throat. I can't swallow. I want to run away to some place—I don't know where.

A part of me still wants to believe that all that had happened was just a nightmare and that it will soon be over the moment I wake up. Unfortunately, I wasn't sleeping. It was all real.

She did say, 'I am sorry, Ravz.'

Those words are still echoing somewhere deep in my ears. They are running in my head, just behind my eyes, and are now flooding out from the corners of my eyes. I am crying and everything in front of me is getting blurred. As I open my mouth to let the pain burst out, the saliva sticks and stretches in between my lips. I let my pain break into a terrible vociferous cry. It was all over. And all that was illuminated in my blurred vigil, through my wet eyelashes, was that date.

24 February. It is today's date, but the trauma it unleashes stretches far back.

Three years back Khushi had left me on this day.

Three hours back Simar left me.

Twenty-six

Those final words of Amardeep brought everyone back to the present. He went numb. No one said anything for some time. After five and a half hours of live reading, a dead silence took over everyone. It was a much-needed silence.

From a distance Shambhavi kept looking at the diary. Her eyes were wide open and they looked heavy.

The overhead light continued to illuminate the table and the faces of all the four people sitting right around it. The rest of the room was dark. And in that surrounding darkness they kept looking at each other. Being a part of the entire narration of the story, Shambhavi more or less appeared to be a part of Ravin's friends. Sometimes this happens. For whatever Amardeep read, Shambhavi could visualize it— she could almost experience the moments from Ravin's life when she touched Ravin's handwriting, when she heard it all from Ravin's friends.

Shambhavi put her hand over Amardeep's fingers which had bunched into a fist. Amardeep struggled to restrain his emotions. Still no one had uttered a single word since Amardeep had ended the reading. The silence continued to persist.

The show was not over—the listeners were still tuned in, hanging on breathlessly. If the technical charts were to be believed the number of listeners tuned in to that show still remained at the same peak as had been scaled in the initial half-hour. It was the very first time that a night show first turned into a late night show and then further ran on to become an early dawn show for the next day. None of the other radio stations broadcasted anything during this time of the day.

A voice shattered the stillness and the quiet in the room. It came from none of the four present. The screen on Shambhavi's display panel had continued to display a never-ending stream of callers and Shambhavi had now accepted one of the incoming calls. That voice attracted everyone's attention, bringing everyone back to the present.

The voice was heavy. It was an old man on the other end. He didn't introduce himself, and neither did Shambhavi ask him to. By now the introduction appeared needless to everyone. Together they were all united as witnesses to Ravin's story.

All that the old voice presently asked was, 'Where is Ravin now?'

Silence followed.

Amardeep flipped the last page of Ravin's diary, closed it and placed it safely in his bag which he then perched on his lap. Manpreet took over the microphone and narrated the part of Ravin's story which Ravin couldn't write.

'You don't always need a madly running truck on the road to kill a love story; many a time people themselves are more than capable of killing their love stories. It was difficult for me to believe that it had happened to him. The most difficult part was to believe that it had happened to him again.

'He was strong enough to bear it the first time when Khushi died in that fatal accident but not that strong to bear it the second time. He broke down. I wondered how he'd survived the first time. He had the guts to share his life's story with the world and then fight against his fate to bring back happiness in his life.

'After Simar broke up with Ravin, whenever I used to call him, I found him lost. One day when I went to Chandigarh to meet him, I was shocked to see him. He was lean and pale. He had huge dark circles surrounding his eyes. His shoulders which used to once be firm and robust now hung low. He hadn't shaved and was wearing shabby clothes.

'As a matter of fact, I didn't even shy away from asking him if he had started doping.

'"Swear on me that you haven't touched dope!" I demanded.

'I was relieved when he assured me that he had not. I tried my best to console him and make him feel better. But I failed. He wasn't ready to come out of it. He told me what all he had been ready to accept for Simar. He recalled how he met her, how beautiful she was and he recalled the good times they had had together. Not that I wanted to hear all that, but he still wanted to share all that. I let him share whatever was making him happy.

'I was surprised when he said that he even went to the nearby gurdwara as Simar had wanted him to do so. Ever since Khushi passed away, he had turned atheist and had stopped praying. All of us had been trying to make him come along with us to the gurdwara, but we failed to convince him. We had believed that he would never again turn up at the doors of the Almighty. We were wrong. He was so madly in love with Simar that he broke his own barriers. All he wanted was her.

'That day, Ravin sat with me for a few drinks in a pub and said to me that even after Simar's denial he and Simar had tried to patch up on a few occasions. Either one of them would text message the other when they were not able to cope with their present situation. On the one hand, he used to cry at night and on the other, Simar too sobbed for him. It was quite unfortunate to know that Simar too was in pain but she would prefer to live that way instead of being rational in her demands.

'As he continued with his tale, he started crying. It wasn't the influence of alcohol. It was the influence of his unlucky fate. He wasn't embarrassed to cry in public. I let him cry. He also talked about having lost in love again, about how true love never comes to anyone the second time.

'I was there with him for two days. While Ravin slept in his room, I met his parents as well. They were terribly worried.

'"I am happy to see you, Manpreet," his dad had said and then asked, "Did he share anything new with you which we aren't aware of?"

'"Nothing as such, Uncle, but I see that he has badly broken down. He was crying some time back." It was all I could say.

'"The difficult time is back again on him and thus on us. Our son is very emotional at heart. After Khushi, how much we tried to convince him to move on. He never wanted to. We forced him. See what's happening now," his mother expressed in a low voice.

'I asked them to be strong and hopeful.

'"Yes, we hope so. *Waheguru sab thik karega*," his dad said and moved back to his room.

'Before I left Chandigarh I learnt from Aunty that Ravin was visiting a psychiatrist and the initial diagnosis of the doctor was not cheerful.

'As I drove back from Chandigarh, I didn't know what to do. All I could do was to hate God like anything. Ravin didn't deserve any of this. All he wanted was to love someone and live his life happily with that special someone. God denied him his love the first time. He repeated his mistake again. Why did God always have to be that cruel to him whenever he wanted to live life? I, for one, don't have an answer to this.

'In the following week I had to leave for the States. I told Happy and Amardeep about Ravin's condition. And the three of us made sure that we would regularly call him up.

'One day Ravin mentioned that he wasn't able to concentrate on his work and that he wasn't able to sleep properly. I could sense that he was gradually sinking into deep depression. His voice was enough to convey that to me. The next time I called him up, his mother picked up the call and I found out through her that Ravin wasn't going to office any more. He had been fired from his job. The reasons were obvious.

'She burst into tears when she told me that the entire day he would keep himself locked in his room. Apparently, not able to see her son in this condition, she called up Simar's family in the hope that something would still work out between Simar and Ravin. She wasn't able to reach Simar and her entire conversation with Simar's family wasn't fruitful.

'Ravin's mental state wasn't okay. He had almost stopped talking and thus stopped taking our calls. He used to get furious at times, especially when his mom would push him to eat his meals. Our only source of information about him were his parents. We were in continuous touch with them and Happy and Amardeep were planning to reach Chandigarh in a week's time.

'But the very next day I had to take that horrible call from Happy . . .'

Manpreet's voice faltered and he started to lose his grip on the subject. He halted for a while and looked at Happy. When he was about to speak the next time, Happy offered to speak instead. Manpreet allowed Happy to take control of the microphone.

Happy began to speak.

'I am sure he would have been in the worst state of mind. All his mom had said to him was, "Till how long will you keep thinking of that girl?"

'To which Ravin replied that Simar would come back soon. He smiled then. His poor mother tried hard to make him abandon his irrational hopes. Ravin kept repeating his words without listening to his mom.

'Unable to tolerate this misery, she slapped him and started crying herself.

'That afternoon Ravin ran out of his house. He ran barefoot on the streets. All he was wearing was a vest and rugged half-pants. He ran without knowing where he was heading. He was as directionless on those roads as he was directionless in his life. He was yelling at his mom, at Simar, at God, at everyone.

'"I don't want to live!" he kept shouting.

'Ravin's dad rushed out of the house in order to follow him. But Ravin continued to run and shout "I don't want to live!"

'A bunch of pedestrians looked at a completely mad Ravin for a while but then finally ignored him. The street merged into the main road, and Ravin ran randomly from one side of the road to the other. There weren't many vehicles on the road but the traffic was nonetheless moving very fast.

'Amid the sound of the moving traffic and the honks Ravin was insanely crying out, "I don't . . . want to . . . This all has got to end! Oh God! This all will have to end!"

'Unfortunately this time his fate tried to fulfil his wish.

'His mad shouting, his wild running and his grief—all ended in one single moment.

'A truck ran over him.'

Happy couldn't say anything for a while. He took a while to regain his strength before he could speak again in his broken voice.

'I hate having to recall and speak all this. But that was the prize of Ravin's pious love. That's what fate had in store for him.

'A bunch of people rushed towards him and circled him. As the eyewitnesses later revealed, our Ravin lay calmly in the dirt of the road. His lifeless eyes remained open for a short while before the scorching sunrays shut them. A pool of his dark blood began to ooze from his body and spread outwards, the dirt floating along with it. His feet shivered slightly but then became still. His clothes were torn and soiled. In that motionless state he still held something close to himself. In the tight fist of his right hand he held those five feathers that Simar had once given him.'

Shambhavi couldn't believe her ears. As soon as she heard this, she put her hand on her mouth.

'God! Is he . . .?' and she wasn't able to complete her question.

Happy continued tonelessly, 'The furious expansion and contraction of Ravin's chest was a signal that he was breathing.

'By then his father had arrived on the spot. People on the road helped Ravin's father to rush him to the hospital.

'Our friend had suffered a fractured skull, multiple brain injuries and a broken shoulder. History had repeated itself in the most interesting but the most atrocious way. Ravin was again in the place he feared the most—the ICU. He mentioned this in his first book. This time he was in a coma.

'The battle between his life and death had started. While each one of us was in the hospital, the girl who he was in love with wasn't even aware of this. Life, at times, gets that nasty.

'A tug of war between reality and hope had started again. Various tests and a few operations, staying back in the hospital and witnessing sad and happy cases of fellow patients, the peculiar smell of medical wards . . . all this had built up enormous mental stress.

'All that Ravin's poor parents could do was pray to God. His brother boarded the next available flight to India. It took Ravin three days to come out of his coma and that was the only time the doctors predicted slightly optimistic chances of his survival. That day we ate well.

'For ten days he continued to be in the ICU. We all were fortunate to receive the final news from his surgeon: "He is doing well now."

'Ravin survived and, honestly, his survival made us forget Simar for a while. It's human nature to assign higher priority to the present problem and push everything else on to the back burner.

'He was later moved to the general ward. All this time we were here in Chandigarh with him.

'Ravin's physical health improved, but his emotional and mental condition still demanded care. As soon as his injuries healed, we found that though his brain was perfectly fine it was under tremendous stress and trauma. Going by the advice of Ravin's psychiatrists and the bunch of doctors at the hospital, it was decided to admit him into a rehabilitation centre in Shimla. It was a tough decision to make. But none wanted to take the risk of letting anything like this happen again in the future. We ourselves visited that place beforehand and found it to be rather nice. It had all the lush greenery you could ask for as well as a conducive environment where various patients could partake in their favourite hobbies. Unlike our preconceived notions of a rehabilitation centre as a place meant for mentally challenged patients, it was a lot different and far more cheerful. This was not meant for people with mental illnesses, but for people who were going through serious emotional stress. I think admitting Ravin there was a wise decision we took.

'Ravin continues to get his treatment in that centre. When I met him last he said, "The Belgian summer has stayed within me and probably always will. I haven't given up. I will soon be all good and I will write another bestseller. You'll see."

'I will never forget what he had said in the end.

'". . . I have two pasts. I don't know which one I should cry more for."

'He laughed.

'I cried and left the place.'

Twenty-seven

That night the *Raat Baaki, Baat Baaki* show ended just before dawn. It was probably the most successful show that any radio channel in the country had had so far. But that's not the only reason the programme would be remembered for. It would be remembered for a heart-touching tale of love narrated live to its audience. For the show itself was a tribute to love and would be fondly remembered for being a wake-up call to the modern-day lovers who have made it a fashion statement to love, break up and quickly move on to find what's next!

For many of us love isn't a commercial commodity. When you say 'I love you' you mean it from the bottom of your soul. When you are promising your love to someone you are promising an entire life to that person. You have got to take all your time and be wise enough before you arrive and commit. You might just be ruining someone's life by breaking your commitment later.

True love is unconditional. And if it is a 'Conditions Apply' scenario, then it isn't true love. It is as good as a mutual fund. And if that is the case then investment in love is subject to market risks and therefore one must please read the offer document carefully. If Ravin could have known Simar's views on marriage in the initial days of his interaction his life would have been different now. Things didn't work between the two of them, because they both loved the same person. He loved her and she loved herself.

As Shambhavi said, it was the best show she'd ever anchored or would ever anchor in the future. For Shambhavi and all the listeners, Ravin's story ended there.

But something else happened after that show in the early hours of the next day. And it was only for Happy, Manpreet and Amardeep that Ravin's story didn't end there.

As the three of them walked out of the radio station, the fog had settled down. But it was still cold. None of them had any sleep in their eyes. They had just relived their beloved friend's life. As per their plan they were to leave for Shimla in the morning to visit Ravin at the rehabilitation centre he was admitted in. They wanted to travel after breakfast and they still had plenty of time on their hands.

Happy suggested freshening up and paying a visit to the gurdwara for the early morning prayers. Amardeep and Manpreet were glad to listen to Happy. The three of them felt the need to visit the gurdwara themselves. As they walked towards their car, they kept thinking about the entire show and all that had happened in the past few hours. They carried a deep satisfaction of having been able to share Ravin's story with the world. They felt strong and united just like they had always been.

The car stopped in the parking lot in the basement. As they entered the courtyard of the gurdwara, they felt heavenly. The sun was yet to rise. The chilly early morning air was beginning to become more pleasant by then. They could sense a divine presence there. As they passed by the sarovar—the sacred waterbody in which a few devotees were immersing themselves as part of the ritual holy dip—they felt at peace, as if everything would be well. They were not talking to each other as they walked inside the courtyard. From inside the sanctum sanctorum the chants and prayers of the devotees took away all their inhibitions and comforted them. They realized that in spite of the low temperature, they were not feeling cold. No one seemed to be feeling the cold, rather—neither the devotees taking the holy dip in the early hours of the day, nor the people walking barefoot in the courtyard.

Once inside, the three of them offered their prayers after which they came out and sat beside the holy sarovar. For a while they kept looking at the holy waters in front of them.

Exactly at that very moment Happy's phone rang. It was placed next to him. Manpreet and Amardeep were shocked to see the name.

It read: 'Simar calling'.

Happy waited for a while and prepared himself to receive the call.

It was a brief call and all he answered in detail was the address of Ravin's rehabilitation centre in Shimla. Happy held the phone for a little while and answered a few questions with a curt 'yes' or 'no'.

The moment he kept down the phone he held his hands together and looked up in the sky. Manpreet and Amardeep, eager to know what had happened, looked at him expectantly. Happy was only too happy to reveal all.

'Last night before we went to the show I had insisted on stopping by at an Internet cafe. And we did stop.'

Manpreet and Amardeep nodded.

'I had emailed Simar the online link of the radio station wherein she could hear us.'

'You mean she heard us?' asked Manpreet.

'She did,' Happy said, nodding.

'I can't believe this!' Amardeep said and jumped with joy.

'It was important to make her put herself in Ravin's shoes so that she could see the situation differently—so that she could see it through Ravin's eyes. Apparently, she wasn't aware of what all had happened to Ravin after they broke up,' Happy explained to Manpreet and Amardeep.

'Indeed, it was important to show her Ravin's part of the story too,' acknowledged Manpreet.

The last thing Happy said was, 'She was hardly able to speak. She took Ravin's address and she kept crying.'

'Hmm . . .' Amardeep acknowledged.

No one said anything after that.

~

That very moment Simar left for Shimla. She drove back to Ravin . . .

Acknowledgements

My sincere thanks to the following people who played an important role in the journey of writing and publishing this book.

Vaishali Mathur, my commissioning editor at Penguin India, for offering me this opportunity. For taking immense interest in this book and being only a call away whenever I needed her. For helping me finalize the title of this book and, most importantly, for accommodating my rigorous schedule at ISB and allowing me reprieve on the submission deadlines. Vaishali, I will always remember our first meeting to discuss this book, when you took me to the CCD in Green Park, New Delhi, because it is blessed with special people who serve there. I was half game to accept your proposal just because of your choice of that place, even though it might have been random.

The very special Khushboo Chauhan, for always being

concerned about this book and asking me plenty of questions. For cheering me up while I wrote some of the key chapters and being ever ready when it came to discussing the ideas of online promotion. You have been my backbone to complete this project.

Dhruv Vatsal, my batchmate and friend at ISB, for capturing, with his camera, the entire phase of my writing this book at ISB, and helping me start my online campaign. The tremendous response that your clicks have garnered over Facebook only further underlines the well-known fact that you are a fabulous photographer.

Shruti Sahni, my fabulous and ever-excited reader, for contributing some of the best lines in this book. For starting various fan pages on Facebook and managing them so well. Shruti, as of today, the fan pages you've created have been 'liked' more than my own! Hats off, girl!

Ambar Sahil Chatterjee, my editor at Penguin India, for cleaning up the mess in my manuscript in the best possible way and, more importantly, for doing it super fast. Ambar, the final manuscript you showed me the other day in the office looked really good.